FAMILY CONNECTIONS

CHRISSIE GITTINS was born in Lancashire and lives in South London. Her award winning stories have been published in magazines and anthologies, and broadcast on BBC Radio 4. Her first poetry collection is *Armature* (Arc, 2003). Her first children's poetry collection *Now You See Me, Now You . . .* (Rabbit Hole, 2002) was shortlisted for the inaugural CLPE Poetry Award in 2003. Her second children's poetry collection *I Don't Want an Avocado for an Uncle* (Rabbit Hole, 2006) was the Poetry Book Society's Single Poet Collection Choice for the Children's Poetry Bookshelf, Autumn 2006. Her plays for BBC Radio 4 include *Starved for Love, Life Assurance* and *Dinner in the Iguanodon*.

CHRISSIE GITTINS

Family Connections

SALT

CAMBRIDGE

PUBLISHED BY SALT PUBLISHING
PO Box 937, Great Wilbraham, Cambridge CB21 5JX United Kingdom

Salt Publishing 2007

Printed and bound in the United States of America by Lightning Source
Typeset in Swift 10 / 12

ISBN 978 1 84471 298 4 paperback

Salt Publishing Ltd gratefully acknowledges
the financial assistance of Arts Council England

1 3 5 7 9 8 6 4 2

For my brother Warren, and in memory of our parents.

Contents

FAMILY CONNECTIONS

IN THE AFTERNOONS EMILY sits by the window in her front room. She cannot understand when she sees a man walk by why he is talking into a remote control panel for the television. Her white eyebrows meet and she cocks her head to one side. Daily she dusts her paperbacks, but now only reads the TV guide and, occasionally, the local paper. On the lowest of her bookshelves are two alarm clocks standing one next to another.

At a twenty past six every day, her sister Connie phones from Great Yarmouth. It's nine years since they last saw each other. Connie used to visit once a year on the train. She'd stay a couple of hours and then go home. On her last visit Emily said, "Oh, you don't want to be bothered. You might get caught up in a strike." She didn't come again.

When their mother died in Great Yarmouth, Connie took over her bungalow. Emily thought she would at least be offered a piece of her mother's furniture, but nothing came her way, not even a vase. The bungalow is now in the middle of a campsite and Connie runs the summer shop.

Emily and Connie were brought up at Forest Hill Swimming Pools. Her father was superintendent there. A first class pool, a second class pool and slipper baths. Each morning before school, the sisters put on their costumes, climbed the stairs to the balcony and jumped off the rail. Blue and green stained glass, Roman numerals on the clock, and the diving board flitted past them before their feet broke the glassy water.

1

Emily often tells her neighbours how they were both in great demand for exhibition swimming, synchronizing their strokes for the opening of new swimming pools. The mayor of Lewisham was mesmerized by their lithe limbs and their perfect poise. Emily swam the channel and won cups. She won medals, cutlery and a silver parrot. Next to the two alarm clocks is a framed photograph of herself in front of a fold-up table which displays her trophies. She's wearing a dark heavy swimming costume. Her commentary to visitors is always, "Navy. It covers your top, your middle, and your bottom."

Emily's family name is King. She hasn't always lived alone, and though she has never been through a marriage service, she has also been known as Emily Day and Emily Hun. Mr. Hun died eighteen years ago. Emily's last birthday was her ninety-second, and she would like it to *be* her last. "I want to go to sleep and wake up dead," she tells her next door neighbours.

Emily rises at five. Each night, before she goes upstairs to bed, she places a piece of white card in her bay window, on the window side of the net curtain. In the morning she removes it. This is a sign to her neighbours that she is up and dressed.

Sometimes Luke and Seth's irritation is mild when they are woken next door by Emily's Saturday morning phone calls, sometimes it's colossal. Eight o'clock, nine if they're lucky. "I've no bread." "My light bulb's gone." "I need my medicine." Emily has no more understanding of an answermachine than she does of a mobile phone. If she rings and gets the machine, then Emily knocks on the front door.

One winter Saturday, Luke and Seth were determined to have a lie-in. Emily couldn't understand why she hadn't seen them. At ten thirty she went out of her front door and stood at the end of the path looking back at the terraced houses. She could see that Luke and Seth's bedroom curtains were still closed. She wavered back into her house and picked up an old Christmas card which she keeps by the phone. In between the holly and robins Seth had written the number of his friend Gill. Gill keeps an eye on Emily when Luke and Seth are away. Emily dialed the number. "There's been an accident next door," she said.

"I'm on my way," said Gill.

Gill let herself into Luke and Seth's place with her spare key. Luke and Seth heard the door opening and quivered in their bed.

Luke is used to the elderly. He runs an office which takes emergency calls—'Life Line'—a service provided to the old and frail for a fairly reasonable fee. "I have never known such kindness," Emily said to Luke once when he made his daily visit. "You and Seth will always be together." To Gill, Emily confided, "They don't have any ladyfriends."

It is Seth who does Emily's weekly shopping. In 1946, after the war, Emily went to see the doctor about indigestion. "Avoid eating anything with pips in it," was his advice.

Since then her weekly shop has consisted of two pieces of skinless boneless chicken (individually wrapped), skinless boneless cod and haddock (individually wrapped), five Mr Kipling cherry bakewell tarts, and two small tins of pink salmon. Seth once bought one large tin of salmon, but Emily rejected it. On a Sunday Emily makes seven lemon jellies with a peach in syrup, resting on a currant biscuit underneath. Once a month she eats four fingers of Kit-Kat.

It was easier when Luke and Seth changed their holiday plans from Greece to the States to let Emily think they were still going to Greece. Luke popped two baking potatoes in the microwave and started chopping red and yellow peppers. "We won't send her a postcard."

"No, just buy her a baklava at that shop in Catford," Seth suggested.

"Don't be mean."

"I'm not being mean. I'm being authentic," bridled Seth.

"She never goes anywhere. Let alone Atlanta." Luke was feeling a twinge of guilt.

"We were going to take her on an outing. The weather *is* getting better. I'll call round this afternoon. See what she says."

"Rather you than me."

The microwave pinged.

"That's not long enough," Seth complained.

3

"I know, I know. I pressed the wrong button."

Seth saw Emily that afternoon over the back garden fence. "Luke's going to call round later on this afternoon." Emily had her hand on the lawnmower. Once a month, on a Saturday, Emily's niece June visited and mowed the lawn. June would push and Emily would walk up and down holding one handle, like a child hanging on to an empty pram.

June's husband sat outside in the car. Some years ago he had borrowed money from Emily and never paid it back. When Emily asked for the money he sent her four shiny sheets of toilet paper through the post.

If either Luke or Seth knocked, Emily was usually at the door like a hawk. But because she was *expecting* Luke she took her time, and limped. "I'm not so well today, Luke. Have you got my medicine?" Emily's medicine consists of foot lotion and a tube of Rinstead pastilles.

"You're not walking so well today."

"What d'you say?"

"Your battery needs turning up, Em." Luke guided her hand onto his forearm and they swayed down the hall. "Where are your batteries?"

"Did you say something?"

"You sit down, Em." Luke held out his arm for her to hold on to as she lowered herself onto the settee. Then he sat beside her and twiddled her hearing aid. "Is that better?"

"Speak up, I can't hear you."

Luke looked around and lifted a china fruit bowl onto his knee. It was full of cotton reels, small white paper bags, shreds of silver paper and a hair net in a cellophane envelope. He picked out a card of small round silver batteries.

"No, not those." Emily picked out a paper bag and pulled out three loose batteries, identical to those on the card. Luke sighed and replaced Emily's battery.

"Is that better?" he asked, adjusting the volume.

"I can hear you now. You're late."

"Did Seth say a time?"

"He said this afternoon. It's nearly night-time."

Luke took a deep breath. "Did he say what I wanted to ask you?"

4

"Not as I remember."

"We'd like to take you out, Em."

"Out! I've not been out in seven years. Properly out. Not counting the doctors and the bank."

"So how about it? Forest Hill Pools."

"The baths? Oh, I don't know, Luke." Emily looked away from him. "Soldiers were billeted there. There were beds the length of the balcony. My father went to war. He walked in after two years and I said, 'Who's that?' My mum slapped me and said, 'He's your father, you little fool.' She turned back to look at Luke. It wasn't the first time he'd heard this story, but he was still struck by its harshness.

"Do you want to see a photo?" Emily darted off the settee and delved into a drawer in the sideboard. She sat down without help and thrust the small black and white shot infront of Luke. The photograph had deckled edges. The image bleached into the white border on three sides. On the back was written in pencil, 'Forest Hill Baths. Coronation. May 12th, 1937.' The front of the building was decked out with lion plaques sprouting flags, arabesques spelling 'GR', banners peeking over the roof, and swags of paper flowers and leaves. "King George VI and Queen Elizabeth," Emily announced proudly. "Of course, we'd moved by then."

"Would you like to see the baths again?"

Emily stared back deep into his eyes.

The day of the outing was as warm as it could be in March. The winter had been mild and as Emily had her strip wash in the kitchen sink she could see that Luke's purple speckled hellebores had half-lifted their faces to show their stamens to the sun. Emily has not had a bath since 1966. She refuses to repair her pipework so she hasn't any hot water. She would rather spend an hour of her day boiling pans and kettles. In her bath she keeps a set of six mahogany dining chairs.

Emily changed out of her tartan pompom slippers and put on her mauve felt hat. Seth pipped the horn and Luke held open the door of the car. Emily struggled with the seatbelt and Seth drove off very slowly. "You all right there, Em?" asked Luke from the back seat.

"Right as I'll ever be," Emily chirped back. They stopped for the roundabout at Sangley Road. "The traffic!" Emily was astounded. "And that's new." She nodded over the road.

"It's a drive-in MacDonald's," said Seth.

"A what?"

"You sit in your car and get served hamburger and chips," Luke explained.

"This is the South Circular."

"Well done, Em," sang Luke. Most of the traffic lights were for them until they reached Forest Hill Station. "A man in a van sells fish here on Thursdays. He comes up from Hastings," said Luke. "Wouldn't suit you, Emily."

The lights changed and they drove along Dartmouth Road. After a slight incline the road dips down and the baths appear on the right—solid red brick and terracotta tiles. Seth pulled over and switched off the engine.

"Oh no!" Luke sank back in his seat.

Over the entrance was a sign in blue letters—'Welcome to Forest Hill Pools.' Over the door and downstairs windows were heavy steel grills. On the noticeboard, written in red it said, 'This centre is closed. Lewisham Direct Team'.

"I've never noticed those griffins on the roof before," said Seth before turning to Emily. Her head was bowed forward and her eyes were closed. Seth gently rubbed her hand to wake her. She did not move.

Luke squeezed forward between the two front seats. When he reached out, Seth handed him Emily's palm. Luke rested two fingers on her wrist and moved them round in a small circle. He couldn't find a pulse. He replaced her hand on her lap and Seth started the engine. The car swung back and round. As Seth reversed into a side street, Emily's body slumped forward. Her mauve hat fell from her head and rested on her feet.

The funeral was very quiet. June came with her husband. When he saw Luke and Seth's loosely tied bunch of blooms on the lid of the coffin, he replaced it with their precision wreath. The vicar stuttered and stumbled on the green grocer's grass which lined the edge of the grave. He thanked Seth, and his wife, for all they had done for Emily.

MATILDA AND ONE OF THE TWELVE DANCING PRINCES

You may remember the King who had twelve daughters, each one apparently prettier than the next. Every night their shoes were danced to pieces. Every morning the servants found them in tatters. The King wanted to know what was going on. He offered the hand of one of his daughters to the first man who could discover where their nocturnal dancing took place. Failure to meant death. Many men tried to discover their secret but were duped by the princesses and lost their lives.

Until one day a soldier came along and tumbled their secret. He had been wounded in battle and could no longer fight. While walking through the woods he came across an old woman. He told her he should like to find out where the princesses danced of an evening. She told him the secret, "Don't drink the wine," and gave him a velvet magenta cloak which could make him invisible.

He went to the palace to meet the King and his daughters. They treated him well enough. The princesses were positively delightful. He was shown the anteroom of their bedchamber and given a futon to sleep on. The princesses slept on twelve pine beds. At the foot of each bed was a pair of soft leather dancing shoes. The eldest princess brought him a glass of wine. She was especially nice. He imagined she felt sorry for him. She must have thought he was bound to die. He remembered just as he raised the glass to his mouth that he wasn't supposed to drink the wine.

He knew he must appear to be asleep, so he lay on his back with his mouth open and made a sound like an intermittent death rattle. The sisters were convinced. They got out of bed and began to dress in their finery and regalia. The soldier, Captain Hugo, put on the cloak which made him invisible. Waiting discreetly until the princesses were dressed, he ventured into their room.

One by one, the princesses climbed down a trap door at the end of the line of dishevelled beds. Hugo crept down after them and almost lost the princesses when he lingered to marvel at the avenues of trees with jewelled leaves of silver, diamond and gold. He caught them up to find twelve princes waiting in twelve boats by the lake. 'They're nothing special,' he thought to himself. He climbed into the nearest boat and soon saw the castle on the island where they danced till three in the morning. 'That's nothing special,' he said to himself.

He went through the same routine for the next couple of nights, following and watching. He was keen to marry the daughter of a King. His family had fallen on hard times and he had three young sisters to support, and an ailing mother. This was his only chance. But his war wounds were starting to weary him and he was stooped with exhaustion. 'I've enough evidence,' he thought. 'I'll go and find the King.' He told the King all he knew and the princesses were paraded into the Great Hall and accused of dancing with intent. None of them denied it. So Captain Hugo was allowed to choose a bride. He plumped for the eldest—Matilda, and they were married that very same day.

The King said Hugo could be his heir. In fact he came out of it quite well, whereas the twelve dancing princes were bewitched for as many days as they had danced nights with the princesses. And how they were bewitched. They walked around in a trance, not knowing day from night. They forgot to eat and do their laundry. They didn't turn up for their appointments with their therapists.

Each sat and dreamed about their particular princess. How they had danced by night on their island, first to rock and Latin, then, as the night grew deeper, Nat King Cole and Perry Como.

Each remembered the lilting rhythms, the soft embraces, the leafy avenues of diamond, silver and gold. They wept and wailed by turn, and grew angry with the soldier who had sussed their nightly sprees.

One prince in particular was in a pretty bad way. His name was Geoff. Not only would he not be able to dance with his beloved, but also she'd been married off to the creep who'd betrayed them. Geoff would go to the shore every night and row to and from the island till daylight. He left the boat sometimes and roamed around the island picking up threads of latex, discarded drifts of swansdown, and leather buttons from dancing shoes. He sang, *When I Fall in Love*, in a flat voice for as long as his weeping would allow him. When he got home he was gaunt and drained. He snatched moments of sleep, only to return again to the shore.

The rest of the crew came slowly back to themselves, carried on with their day jobs—headwaiter, car mechanic, cabinetmaker. They found a club in town and soon forgot about the island. But for Geoff there was no solace. The others tried to cheer him up. They phoned him, invited him out for a drink. But no, Geoff would not be comforted. And in the depths of his misery he conceived a plan.

Geoff knew that Captain Hugo commuted daily from the palace in Sussex to the City. Matilda stayed at home. She was studying for an Open University degree. He would go and see her, and plead with her to return to him. But first he would visit the old woman in the wood. The security at the palace was phenomenal. He was going to need a cloak.

He marched to the woods with a manic energy which delivered him to the old woman's tree trunk in what seemed like seconds. He rapped impatiently. The old woman pulled the heavy oak panelled door towards her and squinted into the daylight. Geoff peeped into her room. The walls were lined with charts of bones and muscle groups, diagrams of astrological houses, and botanical drawings of herbs and medicinal plants. A long leather couch sat uncomfortably against the curve of the trunk. Cardboard boxes were piled high to the ceiling. They held the wrinkles of fairies. The old woman had got rather behind with pressing them into primrose leaves.

"Good Lord," she said when she saw Geoff. "You'd better come in. I've been expecting you for some time, but I'd no idea . . . Your clothes—they're all dirty and torn. When did you last have a shave?"

"I can't remember," said Geoff, slumping on the couch. His eyes were wild with lack of sleep. He told her of his plan.

"Well, you can have the cloak, by all means, but not until I've tried everything I know to calm you down. Lie back and tell me what comes into your mind when you think of the word . . . troubles." She listened to his woes, then she told him to lie on the floor and tense all his muscles one by one.

"That's right. Now your calf muscles . . . moving slowly up your legs, tense up your knees."

She gave him an Indian head massage, then felt the bottoms of his feet. But nothing worked. She gave up, handed him a moleskin cloak, and wished him well.

The very next morning he stole into the palace. When he was sure that Matilda was alone, he slipped into her room. She was watching a programme about aerodynamics. Geoff stood there for a moment and just gazed at her. She was gathered up in an armchair, dressed in silk pyjamas and a fleece dressing gown.

Her hair was newly washed and the damp tufts and curls ranged across her shoulders. All Geoff's anxiety lifted; his skin became clear, his clothes mended themselves, his chin became smooth. When he couldn't bear to be invisible any longer, he dropped the cloak. Matilda dropped the remote control. They fell into each other's arms and didn't move, except to hold on a little tighter.

"Meet me at the boat tonight. I long to be back on the island with you. We were so happy there." Geoff's dancing eyes pleaded with Matilda. She thought it may just be possible. Hugo drank so much when he got back from work that he was usually dead asleep by ten. He said it was to dull the pain from his war wounds, but they both knew they had grown apart. In fact, they'd never been close at all.

"I'll meet you," said Matilda. "I'll be there by ten thirty." Geoff looked enormously relieved. After a further embrace he replaced his cloak and, well, disappeared.

Matilda spent the day anticipating the night. She picked out her earrings in her mind, and saw herself swathed in voile and lace. Her excitement mounted as she sneaked out into the dark, leaving Hugo face down on his bed. She found Geoff waiting by the water in his doublet and hose, with hair gel mussing his fine locks. They kissed four times then took it in turns to row over to the island. There they danced till dawn. The strains of violin and saxophone flexed across the water. Matilda wore sensible shoes for a change and they lasted all of four nights.

It felt strange to be dancing there by themselves. Matilda missed the company of her sisters. The whole thing had a fin de siècle feel about it. But Geoff was oblivious and Matilda didn't have the heart to jar his contentment. They were careful to be back well before the radio alarm went off for Hugo in the palace. It was always set for Radio 4. He liked to check for any snippets on the Dow Jones Index before he left for the office.

By day, Matilda would continue with her studies. She scribed and read and scoured the *Radio Times,* almost with complete concentration. Hugo was absorbed by his paperwork and didn't make too many demands.

Geoff, meanwhile, would row back and forth to the island by day, each time with a different load. He took breezeblocks and parquet flooring, sand, putty and vinyl gloss. He spent long hours at the drawing board, and many more carrying hods, mixing cement and grouting tiles. After several weeks of superhuman activity, he decided to show Matilda his monument.

That night he held out his hand to Matilda as she climbed out of the boat and led her to the far side of the island. He blindfolded her with a pink chiffon scarf, and when they were almost there, he picked her up and carried her over the threshold. Matilda pulled off the scarf and found she was standing in a fitted Swedish kitchen with a double stainless steel sink. She didn't say a word. Geoff took her over the house. Six ensuite bedrooms, William Morris wallpaper, brass bedsteads and deep pile carpet. Spiral staircase, secondary double glazing, sash windows and underfloor heating. Matilda was stunned. She looked aghast as Geoff pointed out his handiwork—dimmer switches, brass door furniture, Roman blinds; swags, drapes and tassels.

In the utility room, Geoff went down on one knee. "Hugo's no good for you, Matilda. He doesn't know you're there half the time. I want you to come and live here with me. There's a fridge freezer full of food, a dishwasher, a bagless hoover and a wide plasma screen digital television. There's a DVD on order and I'll get you any film you want. Oh, and I've got three mobile phones."

"Why three?" asked Matilda.

"In case one goes wrong."

"Geoff, I need some time to think."

"What's to think about?" Geoff thought he'd covered everything.

"Give me a couple of days."

"Alright." Geoff looked sullen.

Geoff stayed on the island while Matilda rowed herself back. Halfway across she stopped and the boat turned gently in the water. Ahead of her the palace was floodlit and looming; behind her Geoff had left the lights on in each room of his dream home. She sighed deeply and returned to her rowing.

As she pulled the water against the oars, a groundswell of emotions began to build from her spleen. First anger, followed closely by intense frustration and claustrophobia. She had married Hugo to fulfil her father's sense of honour. Geoff awaited her over the water filled with a passionate romanticism, which had begun to leave her cold. She began to suspect the leafy avenues of silver, gold and diamond of being paste. Certainly, she could no longer envisage a life-long dutiful marriage to Hugo, let alone being Queen to his King when her father died. And she resented bitterly the ready-made home with which Geoff had presented her. She would like to have been consulted, if only about the shower attachment.

Matilda crept up to her room and collapsed on the bed. She slept late and didn't get out of bed until she had made several decisions. When she did rise from the grey satin sheets, she reached down two suitcases from the top of the wardrobe and packed the bare minimum.

In the coming weeks, Matilda's name and photograph were added to the Salvation Army missing persons' list. A massive search was undertaken. But Hugo and Geoff came to realize that Matilda had probably gone of her own free will, and there wasn't very much they could do about it. They took to meeting up on a Friday night for a drink. They even went to a club.

Matilda herself lives in a pleasant enough studio apartment overlooking Battersea Park. She is beginning to enjoy a measure of anonymity. Her studies are going well and when she graduates she plans to do research into time travel. A lot of her free time is spent on the boating lake in the park. She likes the rhythm of the rowing. She sometimes gazes quizzically at the glistening golden Buddhist temple tiered above the trees. It reminds her of avenues of gold and silver leaves.

TREATMENT ROOM

IT'S A NUMBER FIVE needle I use with you, isn't it? Let me see, where's your card? You started in May. I'd say at least another year, possibly two. I've another client who's much worse that you and I've just got her down from the hour to three-quarters. That was after nearly two years. And you do have a pronounced problem. I'd say we are going to become very good friends.

Now, I always do this side first then halfway through I realize it's worse on the other side. Not too bad today though. But then I always say that.

Had a good week, fortnight? The beauty of this job is that *you* can't speak. You just have to lie there and listen to me. Now, let me see what's been happening. Susie's being a trollop. She winds Neville round her little finger as soon as he comes through the door. She had me up at five o'clock wanting to go out. Been in the airing cupboard all morning. She can reach the doorknob with her paws if she bothers. Then that's her for the day, queening it on the top of my towels. She costs me a fortune. Fifty pounds this week to get her teeth fixed. I don't pay that for *my* teeth. And she won't eat anything out of a tin, oh no! Flakes of cod from Lordship Lane, and haddock if they've got it! But she's beautiful.

My idea of heaven? Sitting with her on the bed while I read a good Patricia Cornwell. I get more affection from that cat than I ever get from Neville. We haven't had a marriage in fifteen years. He won't divorce me. Catholic. I'd better close this door in case he comes in.

His parents are such a pain. They think they can turn up just whenever they like. No phone call. Just turn up on the doorstep. Anyone else would know I can't stand that.

Sorry, it always rings when I'm in the middle of something. "Hello, 815 4324 . . . Yes. Full leg, half leg, bikini. Which did you want? . . . I do an unwinder massage—back, neck and shoulders, a vitamin facial and a total spa. Or you could have a stress buster on a Saturday . . . That's right, you have a think about it. Bye."

Sorry about that, Rachel. I think they just sit at home and ring me up for something to do. Why can't people make a decision before they pick up the phone? There've been a few calls this week. It's always the same when I have new leaflets delivered. It's usually someone asking for a full body massage. Then they slip it in just at the end. "Do you give relief?" The only relief I give is to the taxman. And he certainly doesn't give me any.

There are some strange people. Men seem to like the sound of my voice. They phone up just to hear me on the answer machine. I've been followed down the street by guys who say they just want to hear what I sound like. Generally, I do anyone, as you know—Jehovah's Witnesses, transsexuals, bassoon players, . . . oh, that's you, isn't it.

Transsexuals can be very difficult. There are always complications. And they have to make such a long commitment. You can't really be unemployed. I wouldn't give the discount you're getting to just anyone. You've got to know where you're going in life. What worries me about you is that you know where you're going, but I'm not sure you get paid enough for it. Or often enough. Have you got any more contracts? Blink once for yes and twice for no . . . Three times! What does that mean? Yes and no?

I was talking to my accountant the other day. Roderick. Sorry, did you want to swallow? I'll pull a few of these out now. You're very juicy today. He said there's no point having £4,000 pounds in savings and paying a high rate of interest on my Barclaycard bill. He says I should pay off the card and take out a loan. But it makes me feel secure knowing that £4,000 is sitting there. It's a safety net. I was offered a Platinum card this week. You can't get one if you ask.

You're paying off my monthly payments on the car. So I hope

you're not planning on going anywhere in the near future. That wouldn't be fair. You don't fancy having your veins done as well, do you? Eyebrows? Eyelash tint? Whoops, I've wounded you. First fountain. Stop bloody well bleeding will you!

She drives beautifully. I've another two months, then I have to decide whether to pay the lump sum or sell it. I couldn't go back to an older car. You spend all your money on repairs. Could you slide back a bit for me. That's it. My neck's playing me up.

I can't decide whether to book a holiday. Maybe cross-country skiing? I can't stand downhill. All that palaver to get up the slope just to ski down and then go up again. And I've no head for heights. Last time I went up a funicular I hyperventilated. And it was worse coming down. I just put my head in my hands and hoped for the best. But I thought I might like cross-country —if my thighs can take it. You can't really do it on your own, you have to go in a group. I'd rather be on my own. I don't like people. Nothing personal. But it's not just the holiday. You have to buy all the clothing as well!

I think Roderick fancies me. I've decided men are very strange. A different species altogether.

There you are. I'm quite pleased with you today. Smooth as the bottom of a babe. I've a transvestite next. His kids are going away on holiday and he likes to take the opportunity. He lies here and holds his willy while I wax round it.

❧

Come on up. Oh, could you take your shoes off down here. I've so many of you treading a path. My carpet's getting worn to threads. I'm not wearing my white coat today, I'm being a free spirit. In any case, my coats are all getting tatty and they cost too much.

Do you like my cat drawings and paintings? I've quite a collection now. My niece drew that one. The sun is so bright in here today. I'll close these curtains. Lie down when you're ready. I mustn't forget to start on the other side. Gosh it's bad today. Positive bird's nest! I think we're going to grow old together.

Where do you get your bras from? Do you know you're totally unsupported. You should try getting a proper fitting.

There's a good place in Knightsbridge. I'll give you the address.

I've just had a humus sandwich. I hope I don't smell too much of garlic. Anything I should know about? Got much work coming in? I don't know what you live on. You'll have to come in for a manicure one day so we can have a proper chat. Is that a whitehead there gleaming up at me? I'll cauterise it. There. It should dry up and drop off now.

I've had a terrible week. Three phone calls and two who didn't turn up. You can charge them if you know them, but if they're new . . . Some people make an appointment then they get cold feet. Mind, I had to get rid of my Jehovah's Witness— she was driving me mad. Most people understand that an appointment is on the hour and I need five minutes to prepare and another five to clear away. She wanted an extra ten minutes, free of charge. She was never satisfied. She tried to argue, but I gave her a couple of phone numbers and breathed a sigh of relief.

Men are so predictable. Yes, I am referring to Roderick. It's like an itch they've got to scratch. Once it's over, the irritation stops. I wouldn't mind, but I cooked all this lovely food. Tiger prawns and poached salmon. Champagne. He just wanted to cut to the chase and get it over with. No wonder his marriage is failing. Second marriage. He's no idea. I pity his wife. All the trouble in the world is caused by men. Bush, Bin Laden, Saddam,— they should all be put in a pot and boiled, with salt.

I drove to Yorkshire at the weekend. Mother's birthday. Our Lady of the Jam Jars. I emptied forty-three out of her cupboards into the bin and as soon as my back was turned she took them out again. She's incorrigible. Boadicea in a wheelchair. I didn't know what to get her. They've got everything that opens and closes. I found a nice Hermes scarf in the end. Fenwicks. She seemed to like it. She tied it on to the arm of her wheelchair and said she'd try it on properly later. Father behaved himself, for once. I can't believe he still goes on about the war. He came up through the desert in a submarine and all that. Still, he hasn't laid a finger on her for quite a while now. Once I didn't speak to him for two years. Didn't make any difference. He doesn't know what he's doing. Hang on, I've lost my pedal . . . Got it.

There's a lovely Shetland pony down on the farm there. She is so sweet. Bella. She ate out of my hand and I groomed her—such a darling. I spent hours with her. Had to be dragged away. I wanted to bring her back, but I couldn't fit her in the car and I didn't think Neville would be too pleased. Not that I care. He's going away at the weekend, thank God. I love having the place to myself. I'd live on my own, but I can't afford it.

And it all costs money, you know. That sheet of paper you're lying on. Astringent. Electric current. If this couch goes you'll be lying on the floor for the duration.

I heard some lovely music the other day while I was out in the car. I thought I'm going to buy that. Sound track to the *Titanic*. I know. Why don't I go and get my C.D. player and we can have a listen. Would you like that?"

~

Come up, Rachel. I couldn't be bothered with make-up today. I don't suppose you notice anyway. Don't worry about your shoes. We're moving. The buyers can have the carpets. Tread as hard as you like. I meant to send out cards to let you know, but that would have cost more money.

Looks terrible, doesn't it. Nail varnish, moisturisers, vitamins —all gone. I sold the lot to a stallholder on Deptford market. She'll make a mint. I wouldn't mind, but I've just decorated my bedroom. Duck egg blue vinyl silk. It took me ages to get the right shade.

Comfortable? Then we'll begin. I wish *I* was comfortable. I should have stayed with the Blood Transfusion Service. A nice desk job and a pension. Nights out with the girls and paid sick leave. As it is I pay someone else when I'm sick. My osteopath makes a fortune out of me. I've done my back in leaning over you lot.

And will you listen to that dog. They've locked him in again and gone out. A lovely King Charles. Last time they sent their daughter round afterwards with a balloon on a string for me. As if that would make any difference after three hours of barking. I've a good mind to phone the RSPCA.

And I don't know what you've got to worry about. I can send you to another beauty therapist, but I can't set up another business. You've been costing *me* money. You won't get these prices at Allders in Bromley, you know. Neville says if we get a flat in New Cross we might just manage. New Cross! What am I going to tell my friends? I won't be invited to Henley with an address in New Cross! And if I give a party I'll have to issue bullet proof vests. A flat! One bedroom! Can you believe it? What am I supposed to do with my furniture? I had a quote for my leather three-piece. I might as well cut it up and wash windows with it. One bedroom! Can you imagine? Now I'll have to sleep in the same room as him. He'd better agree to twin beds. And if he thinks he's coming anywhere near me he's got another thing coming!

Damn, I've broken the needle.

PAPERING OVER THE CRACKS

ODETTE BRACED HERSELF AS her copter landed on the roof of the Itex building. There were just two parking spaces left. She folded her blades and taxied backwards towards the wall. As she climbed out onto the tarmac she could see that the Thames Waterway was gridlocked. It was nearly midday, but the morning rush still hadn't cleared. Away to the north the last Green Space was shrinking. Tower blocks were creeping round its circumference, each one higher than the next.

She would soon have to find new premises. Next to the Waterway was a prime location and convenient for everyone in the group, but the numbers were dwindling. It was six weeks since she'd made a profit. Members who had said they would return had not shown up. The reasons they gave seemed plausible enough, but Odette had her suspicions.

She unlocked the door to her suite on the thirty-ninth floor and groaned. The Bubble Club hired this room on Wednesdays and they'd left thirty-two different kinds of new packaging strewn across the floor. As Odette gathered the wreckage into the plastic sack she'd learned to bring along, her group began to arrive. There were brief hellos and acknowledgements, but no one spoke much before the group began. Everyone helped to make a circle of chairs and at twelve fifteen the door was sealed.

Usually a member of the group began, but today was different. Odette didn't want the silence to continue. "So, what's been happening this week?" she prompted.

Francia, a woman from The North began. "I was spat at in the walkpark. I know I shouldn't have made eye contact, but I was just curious. He must have seen my crow's feet when I smiled."

"I was jostled in the cashmax queue," said Marje. "They kept pushing me to the back. It took me two hours to get some money." Marje was in her sixties and from The South. She's had three children by vaginal-birth and ran a night-time nursery. It was usually her neck which gave offence. She had wonderfully high cheekbones, porcelain skin and held herself like a twentieth century classical ballet dancer.

"I've lost my job." Everyone turned to Greg. "They said I either had it done or I was out of the door. They would pay half, I could have time off work . . . They said it wasn't fair on the public—*they* had to look at me every day." Greg was the manager of an old style Novotel. He was a striking man with fierce wavy hair and the skin tone of a forty-five year old. He was fifty-eight.

Everyone sighed. This was becoming a more and more frequent occurrence. Two members of the group had requested demotion to behind the corporate scene in order to safeguard their positions.

"I have a confession," said Dora. She had been unusually quiet. She was the youngest in the group at thirty-two. "I'm not sure I can still be accepted in the group. I took a double lunch half-hour last week and had my teeth whitened."

"Let's see," said Francia. Dora performed a smile. Her teeth gleamed across the room.

"It's all right, Dora," said Odette in a sympathetic tone. "Teeth-whitening isn't listed in the constitution. It used to be. But now it's seen as a minor improvement, along with facials and eyelash curling."

"I just wasn't making my sales targets and I thought this might help." Dora relaxed and sat back in her chair. There was a pause and everyone gave each other the once over.

"Your lips look rather full, Patricia," said Greg.

"I was hoping you wouldn't notice," said Patricia, a heavily made-up woman in her forties.

"Have you had anything done, Patricia?" asked Odette in a neutral tone.

"Just a tiny little bit of collagen. My lips were getting so thin there was nowhere to put my lipstick."

"I'm sorry, Patricia. That really isn't allowed. How can we hold out heads up and support each other if you're using unnatural products?"

"I knew it was wrong. But I work in a cosmetics cubicle! What was I supposed to do!"

Patricia picked up her backsatch and left the room. The door was re-sealed.

"How does the group feel about Patricia's departure?" Odette asked.

As Odette climbed back into her copter she tried not to feel too disappointed. Patricia had been a steady attender and had seemed as committed as the rest. The pressures to paper over and prettify were becoming so much greater.

She rose into the air and got into the anti-clockwise lane. It took her two and a half minutes to get home usually, but nearly four in the afternoon rush. This evening she'd got five friends coming round for dinner. It was actually her birthday, but she hadn't mentioned it to anyone. She looked very young for her age and there was no point in rubbing their noses in it. Most of her friends had been under the knife. That, or bits sucked out and bits pushed in. But if she were as stringent with her friends as she was with her support group, she'd be a very lonely woman. Her current leisure-partner, Tristan, was very supportive—and he seemed to still find her attractive. Even *he* had had his eye bags done for his last birthday.

By seven, Odette had disgorged three courses from fifteen plastic containers and worked out a rota system for her triple microwave. She'd bought a single blue iris—they were so expensive these days—and that took pride of place in the middle of the zinc tablecloth. At six thirty the door tone sounded. Odette assumed it was an early guest and opened the door without checking the camera. Two men stood in foil suits staring straight into her eyes. "May we enter?"

"Well, I'm expecting guests at any minute."

"We will only take a moment of your time. May we enter?" Their tone was flat and they didn't pause between sentences. A chill ran the length of Odette's spine. She'd heard about this sort of thing—an early evening visit, voices without cadence . . .

"Please, do sit down."

"No, thank you. Odette Mainwaring, your activities have been brought to our notice. You must either give up your support group or face the consequences. What is your response?" They spoke simultaneously.

"I'll give it some thought."

"We do not need thought. We do need action. Or rather, in this case, inaction. We prefer to give you the opportunity to desist." They left without ceremony.

Ten minutes later the door sounded again. This time Odette checked the camera. "Tristan, I'm so glad to see you." Odette made to put her arms round him.

"Steady on, Odette. It's not even eight o'clock."

"Sorry, I wasn't thinking. I've been visited." Tristan didn't look surprised.

"You've got to give it up, Odette."

"I can't. I can't let down my members. What would happen to them?"

"They'd have to fend for themselves. Like the rest of us."

"But Dora—she's so vulnerable. And Greg—he tries to be so brave."

"Odette, they're not your children. You have to let them go."

"Maybe if I had children I'd be able to."

"Not this again."

"Yes, this again. Why won't you?"

"You know why."

"I don't think money's got anything to do with it. We're both in part-time jobs! I think you're afraid of growing-up alongside someone who looks younger than you."

Tristran turned to Odette. There was hostility in his eyes. Odette wondered if he'd begun to regret the day they met over the watercooler at their place of work. They both worked for Social Change, doing mainly outreach work.

At the next group meeting there were even fewer members. They rallied as best they could. "I've found a recipe for a face pack," announced Odette.

"Is it on the Net?" asked Francia.

"No, funnily enough, it isn't. I found it in a book."

"Where did you find a book?" asked Greg.

"I found it when I was clearing out my mother's condo after she died. It was buried at the bottom of her health cabinet."

"Is it easy to make?" asked Marje.

"Very easy. You take chamomile, lavender and lemon balm . . ."

"What are they?" asked Francia.

"They're herbs. You have to order them from the cyberstore— they take a while, but it's worth it."

"What are herbs?" asked Dora.

"A kind of plant—they were used for flavouring food, and for medicines. They smell really nice."

"Oh," said Dora.

"Take a handful of each herb, liquidize with two spoonfuls of mineral water, spread it over your face and lie down. Or lie down and spread it on your face!"

"Sounds lovely," said Marje. "I'm going to log it on my phone."

"On behalf of the group," said Greg, "I should like to congratulate Odette on her determination and valour. Over the last few months she has made us see that our point of view is valid and we are entitled."

"Yes, thank you," said Francia. "Coming here has made it possible for me to stick to my guns. I just hope I can keep up my resolve."

"You are very kind. Try to internalise the lessons we have learned here. If we have worked well together then you will be steadfast. Let's chant together—Our Faces and Our Bodies . . ."

The group joined in:

"Our faces and our bodies are our own,
They tell the stories of our lives,
They make us who we are.
We will not deface the passage of time,

We will not pretend to be other than we are,
We rejoice in our years and our wisdom,
We look forward to our futures,
We embrace our uniqueness,
And we will not stoop to someone else's
Image of how we ought to be."

Then everyone cheered long and loud.

The following week Odette was at home boiling the kettle for her mid-morning infusion. She switched on the ten forty-five news bulletin.

Greg Mortimer has been executed for crimes against the state. Odette switched off the kettle. *He was taken from outside his home in Village 3, photographed for the Humanity Museum, and electrocuted. His crime was technological espionage. His remains were disposed of this morning in the tubegrave at Angel on the Northern Line.*

A list of people executed that day followed. Odette switched off the radio. She was devastated. She sank to the floor and stared out of her one window for half an hour. Greg was a good man. He did everything he could for anyone he met. He even borrowed a teddy bear from the parallel collection at the Museum of Child Development to comfort a sick child at the Novotel. Odette wept. She couldn't remember crying since she was a child. When she looked in the mirror her eyes were puffy and red. This made her cry even more.

That afternoon she sent a round-robin laser message to each remaining member of the group saying it was now far too dangerous to go on meeting. She wished them strength and fortitude and looked forward to snatching glimpses of their jowls and dewlaps if they passed each other in the jogpark. It went without saying that they should not, of course, acknowledge each other.

Then she sat down and considered her options. Tristan might not want a child, but she did. She would order a pack of conception pills—she could easily swap them in her dosette for her contra pills. Tristan never came near her without checking that she'd taken them. If she became pregnant and he didn't like it he could apply for a leisure partner transfer. There must be plenty of men out there who would want to bring up a child.

And if not, so be it. Her contract with Social Change was on a rare five-year basis, so she could carry on working.

But she knew that for her contract to be renewed, and for her to attract another leisure partner, she must look her best. She'd heard that Dr Cuticle, a renowned elasticity consultant, was due to visit her local branch of the Royal Cosmo Clinics the following month. She picked up the phone and dialled the clinic's number. "Does Dr Cuticle have any vacancies?"

"He has one appointment left a week on Friday. At nine o'clock in the evening."

She tried to find it in her heart to feel guilty, but that extravagant emotion was remaindered by fear. And a desire that her desire should never go unrequited. The evening of her appointment a cutting wind flew against her cheeks. She thought of her mother and her grandmother—how when she had seen their faces in death, their skin was relaxed and smooth. That was how she wanted to look.

The procedure was slotted in within a week of her initial consultation. The attending nurse tied careful bows down the back of her baby blue gown. Odette noticed there were no windows at all in the clinic. The lighting was gentle and subdued. As Dr Cuticle drew a dotted line with a marker pen along her jaw line, the faces of Francia, Dora, Marje and Greg danced behind her eyelids. Their skin was shining, the lines of their lips were unbroken, their eyes were wide and unblinking.

AMERICAN TAN

Stockings were never long enough. I had the longest legs in my year. I knew because we measured them in gym. We'd huddle in the cloakroom before going next door to the window bars, ropes and vaults. We stood side by side, lifting our games skirts and aligning our thighs. But where did legs begin?

The gap between stocking top and roll-on put more strain on the suspenders than they could take. Strands of vermicelli elastic would escape from the silky band at the top of the suspender. They'd fray and come astray. I hated sewing and mending, so I'd go to school with one or two suspenders missing. If the remaining suspenders were at the front, the stocking would gape down the back of my leg. I'd stand in the dinner queue and yank the stockings up, pulling great holes as my hands ripped through the flesh coloured nylon—American Tan, thirty denier.

One Tuesday I sighed at having ruined yet another pair of stockings as I stood in line for my portion of pink sponge with pink icing and pink custard. Tuesdays started off well— *Bunty* arrived in the morning. I relished the stories and illustrations, but never got as far as cutting out Bunty's clothes on the back cover. The clothes were meant to be attached to Bunty's cut-out figure with fold-over tabs. It seemed a precarious paper-thin way to dress her. And I could never figure out why the Four Marys were always in the third form at St. Elmo's. I always meant to write in to ask, but never did.

But Tuesday was also the day of my piano lesson. The thought made my stomach lurch. I enjoyed the theory. I liked to match the lines of words with the rhythm of the notes. I remembered the Italian instructions—moderato, andante, allegretto. But I hated to play in front of my teacher. And more than that, I hated to play in front of a stranger for exams. I'd sit quaking in the cloakroom at the technical college, feeling sicker and sicker. I'd be called to sit at a grand piano in a vast hall while the examiner lowered his bifocals and ordered scales and arpeggios.

I continued taking lessons, taking exams, sitting in Mr Hamer's back room with its bust of Beethoven and polished wooden metronome sitting on top of his upright. Mr Hamer was very conscientious. Even in a power cut we continued with a candle lighting the keys. But he loved tennis, and when Wimbledon was on he would slip next door to check on progress and scores while I prepared a piece to sight-read.

I sat on the top deck of the bus. It took me past my stop for home. It was two extra stops to Mr Hamer's. I sat in my blue uniform with grey felt hat. The grey hat which at first I'd been so keen to wear. Some girls from the convent sat behind me, giggling. Brown uniforms and berets. They placed some lettuce leaves in the rim of my hat.

The bus pulled up at the stop I needed. As I stood up to go down the stairs I could feel both my remaining suspenders disengage. I stepped off the bus onto the pavement. Both stockings drifted down to my ankles. I wanted to slide down a grid. I hurried across the road to a doorway and pulled off my shoes and stuffed the stockings into my pocket.

I arrived at Mr Hamer's with bare legs and the lettuce still in my hat. We played Scarlatti.

LADY MACBETH

I LOVED MRS MARSHALL. We all did. We wanted to be her. We wanted to be married to her husband and donate our trousseaus to the school play. We wanted a weekend cottage in Troutbeck, and to start our teaching careers in Wales. She wrote notes to herself on the back of her hand; when a member of staff came into the room, we were quiet without being told. I never heard her raise her voice. We wrote poems together, we read Roman myths, we were the last year in our school to parse a sentence.

Each year we dismembered a Shakespeare play. In the first year we read *A Midsummer Night's Dream*; by the second year we were considered ready for tragedy. Books for the year were given out in the first English lesson of the term. Mrs Marshall placed my copy of *Macbeth* face down on my desk. I turned it over and filled in my name and form on the sticker on the inside cover. Above my name was *Sheila Standring LIVM 1963, June Holt LIVW 1964*. Underneath these names *Man from U.N.C.L.E.* had been written in pencil and then rubbed out. The words were lodged in the paper like letters drawn in wet sand. I'd carved *Illya Kuryachin* on my desk the week before and was given an hour's detention. The Deputy Head told me to sand down the desk lid and revarnish it.

We were allowed to take our books home to back with brown paper. We didn't have brown paper at home, so mum helped me cut up remnants of anaglypta and bathroom washable. *A Tale of*

29

Two Cities was covered with scenes from inland China. *From Flints to Printing* was clad in terracotta brick effect. I took the books back to school in my satchel to stack neatly along the bottom of my desk.

The hall was booked for our weekly Shakespeare lesson. We congregated after the bell and waited for Mrs Marshall. Below the high ceilings of the hall were wooden panels and plaques listed with names in gold of old girls and their degree successes. A baby grand piano stood next to the stage. The music teacher played Chopin, Debussy and Clementi as we filed into assembly. After hymns and prayers we listened to a sixth former give a reading from the bible. I dreaded the day I would get to the sixth form and have to read on stage to the rest of the school. Then notices about sports results and societies followed. Once we were warned about putting sanitary towels down the toilet. I sat in horror. How could our headmistress say those words in public? Our headmistress, who had never married because her fiancé was killed in the war.

"Get the benches out please, girls. Three in a triangle," said Mrs Marshall. We dragged out benches from piles stacked at the sides of the hall and arranged them on the parquet floor. The parquet floor where we knelt at the beginning of each term to have the length of our pleated skirts checked. The floor where we stood waiting for assembly to start and whispered the latest gossip.

"Have you heard about Mary Bennet? She's got to leave." I didn't believe it. She was a prefect!

We sat silently on our benches. It was a single lesson. At break-time I had huddled with Karen and Sandie in a snigger over the desks in our form room. Sandie pointed to a worn page of the play. "Have you seen what she says?"

"Who?" I asked.

"Lady Macbeth."

"Where?" said Karen.

"Page 66. And page 71—that's even worse." We read it over Sandie's shoulder and winced.

"I'm not reading that," announced Karen.

"Neither am I. No chance," said Sandie.

As we sat attentively, Mrs Marshall asked who'd like to read parts. She cast the parts as we read scene by scene. First the witches, then the men with names like Scottish biscuit manufacturers—Duncan, Lennox, Donalbain. All hands shot up to read the King and Banquo. At the end of Act One, Scene Four, there were five minutes of the lesson left.

"We won't start another scene just now," said Mrs Marshall. "But who would like to read Lady Macbeth next lesson?" A long thin silence zipped along the benches. Eyes dropped, legs crossed and uncrossed. The fingers on the clock ticked past the Roman numerals. Mrs Marshall looked around. Mrs Marshall who smiled and said hello to everyone, even off school premises. Mrs Marshall who was patient with late homework and ran the Busy Bee Club for sick animals in her lunchtime. She must realize what she was asking someone to do? The silence grazed a little further. I couldn't stand it. I put up my hand.

At lunchtime I stood with Karen and Sandie in the corridor. Our form teacher, Miss Bickerstaff, walked down the staffroom stairs. She had natural white-blonde hair and wore neat skirts. Her subject was Latin. "I'm going to ask her," said Karen.

"Ask her what?" I said.

Miss Bickerstaff smiled at us as she walked by.

"Miss . . . ?" said Karen.

"Yes . . . ?"

"Can you tell us what a Latin word means?"

"What is it?"

"Coitus interruptus."

Miss Bickerstaff paused and scrutinized our facial expressions. "If you promise to take it seriously."

"We will, Miss."

We followed her into our form room and closed the door. We left the room ten minutes later. I felt sick.

When school finished that afternoon I tucked my copy of tragedy into my satchel. I wasn't sure if my best friend was still my best friend, so I didn't wait for her and walked to the bus stop alone. Valerie and I had started to be friends in the first year. One break time over the book cupboard she said, "I like you. Do you want to play jacks?" We played jacks endlessly— throwing the ball, snatching the metal stars with the same hand, then catching the ball on the drop from its bounce. I stuffed them back into my hand-made drawstring bag when break was over. Valerie came to my house, I went to hers. But then Jane came along and that changed things. Jane joined the class in the middle of the year. Valerie began to spend more time with her than me and I pretended not to care.

At home I had tea with mum, and after written homework I took the key to the caravan and went into the garden. I hated caravanning. It felt like living in a vacuum flask. We would sit around the drop-leaf table listening to the rain pelting against the roof, as the smell of the chemical toilet seeped from behind its door.

One winter's night the caravan was broken into while it stood at the top end of the garden on its concrete base. The next morning we found a sleeping bag from one of the cupboards curled up on the narrow bed. I was glad someone had stolen a good night's sleep.

Sitting at the table, I looked at Lady Macbeth's speeches. I ran my finger along each line and read out loud until my intonation made sense of the words. I read slowly and deliberately. When I felt at ease with the words I closed the book, locked the caravan and went back inside the house.

"What have you been doing?" asked mum.

"Nothing."

It was double English the next morning. When the bell sounded for the end of break my class ran along the corridors to the hall. We were told to "Walk, girls. Keep to the left." We dragged out the benches and were sitting squealing and shouting when Mrs Marshall appeared at the double doors. "Girls, girls! The bell's gone. Other classes are trying to work." She paused. "Thank you for getting out the benches. Let me see everyone sitting quietly." She paused again. "Good. I haven't any homework to return to you today so, Amy, tell us what's happened so far in the play."

Amy was quick with her answer. "There's a battle, Miss, and Macbeth and Banquo come across three witches on a heath. They say that Macbeth will be king."

"Yes. Thank you, Amy. Are we ready? Act One, Scene Five." Mrs Marshall nodded towards me.

I read Macbeth's letter to Lady Macbeth and raised my voice

slightly. At the end of the page everyone turned together. Even Rosemary Bell was on cue. She usually gazed out of the window when we were reading. When the messenger arrived there were one or two shuffles as everyone sat up or leaned forward a little. Then the messenger left. I took a deep breath.

"Come, you spirits
That tend on mortal thoughts, unsex me here
And fill me from crown to the toe top-full
Of direst cruelty. Make thick my blood;
Stop up the access and passage to remorse,
That no compunctious visitings of nature
Shake my fell purpose, nor keep peace between
The effect and it. Come to my woman's breasts
And take my milk for gall, you murdering ministers,
Wherever, in your sightless substances,
You wait on nature's mischief."

I could feel my neck redden, but my voice did not falter. We continued without discussion. At the end of Act One, Mrs Marshall looked at me and said very quietly, "Good." She never gave easy praise. The class sat very still, and stared.

A SMALL SMUDGE OF BLOOD

THE FIRST TIME I felt a penis in my mouth was in a field on a Friday night. It was June. Martin had grown bored with my inexperience. Was I supposed to swallow it? It tasted bitter, like a milk pudding gone sour. His friends along the field heard it first —the grass had rustled. We'd disturbed a bull. The barbed wire was low enough to climb, but not to jump.

A week later we sat on his parents' settee. It was brown and itchy with black twists of wool growing through the cushions. "I've waited three months," he announced. Was that how it was? Was I supposed to be grateful that he'd waited? I didn't know the rules. I didn't know there weren't any rules. I wouldn't have minded, but it was his friend I fancied—Simon Christmas. He had thick, dark, curling hair, like a bending athlete on the side of a Grecian urn. Martin got to me first at a party. He had a beard. He had a job. He earned money—as a systems analyst at the C.W.S. building in Manchester. He sat me on his knee, very pleased with himself. "I can go to ten parties and not find anyone I like." I hadn't yet got the habit of parties.

At school I liked art lessons best. It was the only time we didn't have to sit in silence. In Art we could talk behind our wooden drawing boards. We'd be painting on the theme chalked on the blackboard—'Autumn Leaves' or 'Cats on Dustbins'.

"Mandy has," said Julie.

"No!" I said, amazed.

"So has Elizabeth."

"Elizabeth?" I was shocked. Elizabeth was my first choice for head girl. I didn't know if I could still nominate her now.

"Her and Barry have been doing it for ages."

"Where?" I asked.

"They drive to Redisher Woods and walk for a while with a travelling rug."

I wasn't quite sure how much to believe. But as we scraped the hog hair brushes across the round blocks of poster colour, we took a weekly tally. If what they said was true then I was in the minority. I would sit on the bus going home trying to imagine how it would feel to be one of the majority. How would it change me?

Meanwhile, Martin and I sat on his parents' settee. He guided my hand to the mound in his trousers and unfastened his zip. The carriage clock ticked away on the mantelpiece. His parents looked out blankly from a gilt frame. 'Wedding Day' was written in sweeping arabesques of white ink along the bottom of the photograph. His mother looked particularly puzzled in her white veil and fitted frock. Afterwards Martin just sat and smiled at me for a long time.

A week later, along the railings near my house, Martin pressed up against me. It was a chilly September evening and we had walked back from a pub in town. The iron bars made ridges in my back. Martin sighed deeply and pulled away. "Let's get married," he said. I didn't say anything. I was about to go to university. I couldn't marry a boy from Bury who proposed to me up against the railings of the Lido. Martin buttoned his corduroy jacket and walked me round the corner.

In October I arrived in Newcastle with my trunk. My digs were on a bleak council estate in Denton Burn. I was sharing a room with Annie from Worcester. We would lie on our small parallel single beds reading *The Eye and the Brain* and *Tamburlaine*. Outside dogs barked endlessly.

Our landlady was Mrs Gallon. Her husband was away at sea and she talked us to death morning and night. She cooked breakfast every morning with black pudding and fried bread, and she made our tea—plate salad with balls of cold potato mashed with cheese. By the second week I had fleas from Lucy the cat. It wasn't quite how Annie and I had envisaged university life. We began to skip tea and eat at the university refectory.

I didn't hear from Martin. After two weeks I chanced the rain one evening and stood in the dark in the only phone box on the estate. The raindrops on the glass drizzled into each other and ran the length of the window. I dialed the number. Martin picked up the phone straight away. "I'm really glad you phoned. I didn't know what to say." Why didn't he know? Did I know any better? We talked for a while till the distance fell away.

"I'm coming home in two weeks. For a weekend." It didn't seem too long to have to wait. I wondered what it would be like to see him, to feel the toughness of his beard, to have him want me again.

The journey home dragged. I phoned Martin as soon as I'd taken my bag upstairs. We arranged to meet the next day, Sunday. Then I realized that if I invited him for dinner we would have more time together. I asked mum. She was peeling and coring apples in the kitchen. She looked up and paused. "Go and ask your father."

I walked down the stone steps, past the frayed stumps of rhubarb, the dripping fuchsia and the late bitten roses. Dad was repairing the fence. "Can Martin come for dinner?"

"No." He didn't even stop hammering.

I walked back to the house. Mum was lining a dish with pastry. The lino on the floor was newly washed and stuck with sheets of newspaper. "He said, 'No'." Mum went on shaving the pastry from around the top of the dish. I went upstairs to my room.

If dad wouldn't have Martin in the house, then I would go with him outside the house. I packed my case and called him. When I heard the moan of his Morris engine I ran downstairs. I didn't say goodbye to dad. Mum stood in the hall, the white banister stretching up behind her, wringing her floury hands. "Just drive," I said to Martin. He headed for Manchester where I could get my train. Mum and dad never said they didn't like Martin. The only thing mum would say was that she thought it was rude to walk into a room and switch on the television without asking.

We sat in the station buffet. Every few minutes a head of steam lifted from the silver hot water urn at the counter. I sipped my hot chocolate and looked at Martin. I'd wanted to see how it felt with him—then I would know whether to carry on. That 'No' of dad's had brought us closer. I would go on seeing Martin. I would go on having a boyfriend at home. We found the platform and I found a carriage. Martin waved, unsmiling, as the train drew away.

It stopped at Staylybridge, Mossley, Greenfield, Marsden, and every station between Huddersfield, Leeds and York. The carriage was musty. The paintwork was dark brown and the seats were scratchy. Above the seats the lights flickered three times then died. As the train rushed through the darkness and the scattered lights of kitchens and petrol stations, I sat upright, expectant. Annie and I were planning on leaving Mrs Gallon's. We were going to get a flat-share. I would ask Martin to come and stay. It was time. I wanted to know.

Annie and I found a postcard on the Union building notice-board—an upstairs flat in Heaton. It was on the top floor of a red brick terrace—dark and narrow with turquoise woodwork on the landing. There were three bedrooms—medium-sized, very small and even smaller. Dave and Anna, who had advertised for sharers—third year French—had the larger room. They pushed their single beds together and asked the landlord for a double. It never arrived.

Though strangers to each other, we lived communally, taking turns to cook in the evenings. Anna grated carrots for rapée, Annie added double cream to macaroni cheese to make it 'de luxe', I made chilli con carne with tins of baked beans.

My room was loaded like a furniture van. Piles of clothes marked out the purple carpet. I tidied-up for Martin.

We met at the station and went across the road to Yates's Wine Lodge. The bar was loud and dense with smoke. Men who'd left their homeland and families to build roads and bridges were singing in Gaelic and reeling towards the bar. We drained our sweet syrupy wine and walked the shiny streets to the bus stop.

The flat was quiet. No one was back. We made tea in heavily patterned mugs and went to my room. Without speaking we undressed ourselves and lay down facing each other on my narrow bed. Too soon he came inside me. For a moment I felt filled-up, complete, but none of the luscious sensations I'd been expecting. He pulled away from me and slept. I lay awake, not understanding.

As we walked round W.H. Smith's in Eldon Square the next day, I remembered the night before. There'd been a slight rip of pain, then a gash of disappointment. I needn't have waited. After Martin left, I cut out a square of the bed sheet where there was a small smudge of blood. I kept it in a pale blue jeweller's box along with an old eye-tooth and a locket I'd been given as a bridesmaid.

We saw each other next at Christmas. There was an afternoon when my parents were going to be out. "You know why I'm coming round, don't you?" Martin said. It felt like a threat. We lay on my childhood bed and he came in my hands. "Sorry," he said, "I got too excited."

Downstairs we began to kiss again. Between the settee and the armchair, on the floor of the sitting room, I began to feel pleasure. He held me hard against him until my shudders subsided.

Seven days later my period was due. I sat around the house with a jab of anxiety in the pit of my stomach. Every half-hour I went to the toilet to check. "What's the matter?" asked mum.

"Nothing."

Martin seemed unconcerned. This had happened to him before and the girls were never pregnant. He was beginning to think he might be infertile. I think he wanted me to prove him wrong. I began to hate him.

After nine days I started to bleed. In the relief I told mum what had happened. "I know", she said. The same thing had happened to her, except that she *was* pregnant. She married under a girder of disapproval. She married in a powder blue bararthea costume with a white satin hat and tan shoes. There was a spray of orchids in her lapel. They didn't tell the staff at the hotel in Morecambe that they were on honeymoon. But mum said they knew because at breakfast she had to ask dad if he took sugar in his tea.

I never saw Martin again. That January he sent me a present for my birthday—the *Penguin Book of English Romantic Verse*. In it he wrote that I'd been too full of romantic images for him. The day I got back to Newcastle for the spring term I made an appointment at the university clinic. I wanted family planning, without the family.

THE UNDERSTUDY

IN FRONT OF BILL was a hoarding filled with a black and white photograph of an elderly couple looking miserable. It was an advert for Thompson's holidays. The caption read, 'Remember that time we nearly went to Istanbul?' Bill shuddered. He hoped he wouldn't live out *his* days in regret—though Istanbul had never particularly appealed to him. He'd once been offered free tickets for a week in Paris, but he didn't take them up. For one reason, his white irises were just about to come into flower and he really didn't want to miss them; he'd also done all the travelling he wanted to do in the war, thank you very much. His wife didn't seem to mind. Or, if she did, she never complained.

The platform was coated with scattered snow. It had been a bitter winter and Bill was looking forward to spending more time on his houseboat in Shoreham. As it was, he must take the train one more time—Sydenham to London Bridge, change to platform six for Charing Cross.

He liked to look at Tower Bridge as the train roared through the city. If the sun shone then the two gold finials would glisten. He liked the way the train ran halfway up and bang next to Southwark Cathedral. Then he could look down on Nelson Mandela cut off at the breastbone on the plinth outside the salad bar of the Royal Festival Hall.

Yet again, there was no one to take his ticket at Charing Cross. He realized he was lucky not to have to travel during the rush hour. Today was Tuesday matinee—he could set off just after lunch. And for evening performances he travelled up town as the commuters were on their way home.

As long as he was in the theatre by one forty-five then his slate was clean. Not that he'd ever been late, not in fifteen years — so why worry now? Well, that would be the tip of the iceberg. It might be his last day, but if he started to cut corners where would it end? He took after his father. His father was a man who made certain conditions when Bill was a boy before he was allowed to join in their Sussex village carol singing. "Are they covering all the four-part harmonies?" he would ask each year.

"Yes, Dad."

"Then you may go." And off he would walk, swinging a jam jar by its string handle, a lighted candle warming his glove.

He'd had four days off in 1987 when he'd succumbed to a particularly vicious strain of flu, but thankfully the weekend was enough to get him back on his feet. And apart from a day off for his wife's funeral, he'd been as constant as his mauve alpine clematis which flowered every May. He turned the corner off St. Martin's Lane into West Street. The red neon sign 'AGATHA CHRISTIE'S "THE MOUSETRAP", 45TH YEAR' was flickering. 'There must be a technical fault,' thought Bill. 'I'll mention it to Joy when I go in.'

Next door at the Ambassadors Theatre a new play was showing. It was called 'Shopping and Fucking.' Bill hadn't seen it. It was having quite a long run, and whenever Bill arrived there were always several young men with very short hair and hats standing in front of the theatre. They would all be facing different directions and talking into mobile phones. In a copy of *Time Out*, which Bill had found on the train recently, he noticed that 'The Mousetrap' was billed as 'booking till Domesday'.

Bill opened the St. Martin's Theatre stage door and gave Joy a wave. Joy was 'back of house'. Her tiny office was no more than a cubicle painted with black gloss paint; enough room for a television, a telephone and a kettle. She was there before the performance started and she left after it had finished. Her flat was along the far end of The Strand. She could just make it home in her break, but by the time she put the kettle on it was time to set off back. Joy already knew about the flickering lights.

At the bottom of a flight of stone steps, a door led backstage.

There was a new understudy struggling with the sound equipment. They could pick up a bit of extra money that way. The young woman who was understudying Miss Casewell assisted the assistant stage manager. "How are you doing?" asked Bill.

"I'm having trouble with the police bells and the piano music. They're in the wrong sequence." Bill left him re-winding and fast-forwarding his tapes, his index finger scanning the script. He wanted to stand on the set one more time before the curtain went up.

Beside the steps up to the stage was a wooden wind machine. Bill turned the handle, gently at first then more fiercely. The canvas rattled on the surface of the drum till it wound down to a breeze. Detective Sergeant Trotter's skis leaned in readiness against the back wall of the set of Monkswell Manor. Bill could hear Trotter saying his line, 'As I can ski, they sent me'. The canopy, which hung above the back of the stained glass window, had been re-filled with 'snow'. Pieces of flock were poking out of the hundreds of tiny slashes in the canvas, waiting to be released with a swaying motion at the beginning of Act One.

Bill stepped up onto the set and stood on the Persian carpet next to the fireplace. He was the understudy for the part of Major Metcalf. In fifteen years he had played the part on only a handful of occasions—a broken leg, a heart attack and a couple of bereavements. Each time the cast was renewed there were rehearsals for the understudies. Then he got to wear his thick tweed suit and polished brogues. Otherwise, the suit hung in the understudies' wardrobe.

He played Scrabble with the other understudies during the performance. He would listen to their aspirations—to sing in a Lloyd Webber musical, to be a major player in a season of Brecht, to be in anything which opened on Broadway. Bill supposed he must have had ambitions when he started out, but he couldn't remember what they were. It had all been such a struggle that when this job came up he grabbed it by the throat. The way he saw it, he could still call himself an actor and he didn't have to stack supermarket shelves.

A rocket-engine gas cylinder was shooting heat into the auditorium. Bill went along the mantelpiece inspecting the row of jugs. Only the largest had a trademark—Mason's Ironstone

China. He remembered how the Mrs Boyle from the previous cast would go through this ritual when she was on stage, picking up each jug in turn and shouting, 'Rubbish!'.

Bill heard footsteps from the other side of the stage and looked over his shoulder. Molly, who played the current Mrs Boyle, strode towards him. She played him a line from the script. "'Would you mind shutting that door, this place is full of draughts.'"

Bill chuckled. They often quoted their own lines out of context to each other. "Last day today," Bill reminded her.

"'Well, I consider this an impertinence. It is melodramatic nonsense and I don't believe a word of it.'" They both giggled.

Molly had been part of the company for eight years. It wasn't many months till her own retirement. She was married to a significant civil servant and lived in relative luxury in Chelsea. Molly often chatted to Bill about her grandchildren—she was triumphant when her son was called to the Bar. But she never talked about her husband. Bill found her in tears one afternoon in the foyer. She looked down at the maroon carpet and said something which Bill couldn't quite make out, but which included the words 'mistress', 'young researcher', 'setting-up home' and 'Muswell Hill'. In the months which followed, neither of them referred to this conversation.

"How about a drink after the second half?" asked Molly. Mrs Boyle was killed off just before the interval, which left her free till the final curtain. She sometimes nipped out to do a bit of shopping around Seven Dials. There was a flower stall there called the Wild Bunch which she particularly liked, and then it was only a spit to the Neal's Yard cheese shop.

"Well, since you can't make my send-off party—I think that would be a splendid idea."

"My dressing room after curtain-up?" suggested Molly.

She went off stage right and Bill stood for another few minutes in the formal majesty of Monkswell Manor. It hadn't been a bad life. A steady income, the camaraderie of his colleagues, the gratification of being part of an edifice of British society. Granted, the cast didn't always play to capacity audiences, but a forty-five year run was quite an achievement. He felt he could walk out of the theatre that afternoon with a sense of satisfaction. No, he wouldn't have done it differently. It was sad that his wife wasn't with him in his final years, but he was constantly reminded of her—in the curtain material she chose just before she died, and in their garden on a south-facing slope which they had tended together for so many years. 'Over these things one has no control,' Bill often said to himself.

When the audience had settled to the second half, Bill went along to Molly's dressing room. He knocked and opened the door gently. The centre light in the room had been switched off —all that remained was the frame of light bulbs around the mirror. Molly was sitting on an upright kitchen chair in front of the mirror. She was completely naked. Bill saw the ivory of her back and the outline of her elegant shoulders. In the mirror, Molly's eyes lifted to meet Bill's. She tried not to show any emotion— she wanted to judge Bill's reaction. Bill stepped back outside the door and closed it gently. He was shaking slightly. He liked Molly very much, but he couldn't do this; he hadn't touched a woman since his wife died six years ago. He decided for once that he would not wait for the final curtain before leaving the theatre. The air outside was sharp. He could pick out the footprints in the snow which he had made when he arrived.

As he stood on the platform at Charing Cross, he wasn't entirely sure when the next train was due to arrive. His routine had been thrown out of kilter. To his surprise, Bill didn't find this as unpleasant as he might have expected. He went over in his mind what had just happened. As well as being shocked at Molly's overture, he was also a little flattered. Molly was a fine woman—in her way. Even so, he was glad that it was unlikely he would ever see her again.

When the train arrived he walked further down the platform and chose a carriage which was already full. His inclination was usually to be solitary. As the train pulled out, a tall fair woman made her way through the carriage looking for a seat. There was a space opposite Bill. She wedged herself between two shoppers and placed a carrier bag carefully in the space between Bill's suede slip-ons and her leather loafers.

Bill noticed that she had a dark freckle on the upper side of her left cheek—in exactly the same place his wife had had a 'beauty spot', as she called it. The line of the woman's mouth was slightly puckered and her eyes were a clear aquamarine. She looked out of the window as the train sailed over the river. The slats on the side of the bridge flicked shadows across her face. At Waterloo East, Bill tried not to watch her as she pulled a booklet out of her carrier. It was a Sutton's seed catalogue.

At Honor Oak she stood up to get off. Bill caught her eye and smiled. The doors clamped shut and the train picked up speed. Bill strained to see her as she walked towards him up the platform. She was smiling. He waved too late for her to see him.

He checked the time and made a mental note of the position of his seat in the carriage. When he left the train at Sydenham, he counted down the number of carriages from the engine to the one he'd travelled in. 'Fifth one down,' he said to himself. 'I must remember that. Fifth one down.'

STEPPING IN THE DARK

AT THIRTEEN, JULIA WANTED her mother to die. She woke up in a friend's dawn bed. The pain of the guilt cracked into tears. Her friend woke up. "What's the matter?" asked Janice. Janice and Julia were holiday friends. Janice lived in Manchester and Julia lived in Rochdale. They visited each other at Christmas and Easter. In the summer their families camped and caravanned together in Anglesey and Pwllheli. In term time they wrote to each other on pastel-coloured notepaper. Julia was staying over at Janice's for her thirteenth birthday party.

"I wished my mum was dead." Julia sobbed bitterly, but thought she did not deserve any solace this confession might bring.

"Shh," Janice soothed, finding Julia's hand under the covers. "It's alright. You didn't mean it."

And she didn't. But she didn't know that then.

Two months earlier, Julia had woken in her own bed in the middle of the night. She could hear shouting. She pulled back a corner of the curtains. The crab apple blossom hung below her window like halted snowflakes. When this tree was in flower her mother called it Julia's bridal bouquet. Julia had no intention of getting married.

"I can't do it any more!" It was her mother she could hear shouting downstairs. "And why do we never see your brother from one year to the next?" Her mother's voice was strained and several tones lower than usual. She sounded like a different person. Julia had never heard her shout before.

She sat up in bed and pulled the cord on her reading light. The twelve foreign dolls on her chest of drawers looked anxiously across at her. The Spanish dancer with his arms outstretched, ready to click his castanets, cocked his head to one side. The alarm surfacing inside Julia made her sob. 'Maybe if they hear me crying they will stop,' she thought. The shouting carried on.

"And why didn't we get a wedding invitation from him? It was your niece's wedding!" The event was three years ago. She could hear her father speaking in gentle tones but she couldn't make out what he was saying.

'Perhaps if they see that I'm upset they will stop,' thought Julia. She climbed out of bed and walked to the top of the stairs. The carpet chafed her bare feet. As she went down the stairs she ran her hand along the raised surface of the bamboo-effect wallpaper. The bumps and valleys were familiar to her fingers.

The sitting room door was open. Her mother was sitting on the two-seater lilac settee, her face a screw of tension. Julia's father was standing in front of the television, his arms folded across his wide chest. He looked tired and bewildered. Julia sat on the settee and took her mother's hand in hers. It was cold and clammy. She looked into her mother's eyes and saw fear and anguish. "It's alright, Mum," she said, "God loves us." She'd given up religion the previous year, but it was the only thing she could think of.

When Julia remembered this night, she realized it was the culmination of a series of peculiar incidents. A blue metal vase encircled with two snarling dragons had disappeared from the mantelpiece in the sitting room. A set of six silver teaspoons hanging on a silver stand had gone missing from the breakfast room. Both these items had belonged to Julia's grandmother— her father's mother.

"Where did this vase come from?" Julia asked her mother one squally day when it was too wet to wander outside.

"Dad sent it back from India when he was in the forces. It was one of a pair. But the other never arrived. Your grandma gave it to me a year after we were married. Dad posted a couple of carpets too. God knows where they got to. She gave me those teaspoons as well. They've got an 'S' engraved on each handle. Did you notice? "

"Yes," said Julia. "Why do they have an 'S'? Our surname begins with 'F'!"

"Grandma won them in a tombola. A very exclusive tombola, she would have me know."

"Did you like grandma?" Julia asked.

"She didn't like me. I wasn't good enough for your father."

"Why not?"

"Being pregnant with you didn't help. Your father didn't tell them. They found out from someone else. Wouldn't come to the wedding. You were four weeks old before they saw you. And then they only came because you were very poorly."

Julia found the vase and the spoons six weeks later. Her mother had hidden them in the cupboard under the stairs when she couldn't bear to look at them.

The night before the shouting night, Julia's mother had gone next door to see the neighbours. She didn't usually visit the neighbours. Mr and Mrs Stumblich were kind enough. They had a son who'd been hit in the eye with a stone as he walked home from school. His left eye was now a ball of unmoving, unseeing glass. Julia's mother would tell this story to visitors—but this was the only way the Stumblich family featured in their day-to-day lives.

The day after the shouting was the last Friday of Julia's Easter holidays. Her mother ran outside into the street in her apron shouting, "Leave me alone! Leave me alone!" She refused to come inside. Standing on the opposite pavement, she held on to the iron railings which were rooted in a low stone wall.

"Julia," said her father, "I want you to go to the surgery. Tell Dr Stuart what's happened." Julia wanted to help, but she was terrified. How could she explain to anyone what was going on? She ran to the bus stop and hailed the orange double decker. It drove past the park and the youth club, past the parade of shops with The Friary chip shop, and past the chiropodist where she'd had her verruca removed. She got off at the stop outside the surgery. The receptionist sat peering out above her spectacles.

"What can I do for you?" she asked.

"Can I see Dr Stuart? . . . Please."

"And you are?"

"Julia Fell."

"Are you registered with Dr Stuart?"

"Yes."

"Do you have an appointment?"

"No."

"Take a seat. Surgery's almost finished, but he should be able to see you." She smiled warmly at Julia.

The receptionist didn't seem to think it was strange that Julia was alone, or if she did, she wasn't showing it. Julia sat down on a grey plastic chair. She was shaking. What was she supposed to say to the doctor? How could she convey to him how upside down everything had become? Time had taken on a new meaning, or no meaning at all. Everything was happening slowly at her house. Her father tried to do the cooking, but he burnt the lamb chops. They didn't see anyone from morning to day's end. And nothing actually happened. The grass didn't get cut, the car was dirty, the washing wasn't hung out. She tried to steady herself by reading the notices on the wall. Heart Disease. Antenatal Classes. VD Clinic. Then Dr Stuart appeared. "Julia Fell?"

Dr Stuart arrived at the house twenty minutes after Julia got back home. She saw his blue Rover pull up from the front window. Her mother had come back as far as the garden wall, but refused to go any further. Dr Stuart put his hand on her shoulder. "Hello, Mrs Fell. How are you?"

"Hello, Dr Stuart," said Julia's mother said brightly. "I'm very well. How are you?" He smiled at her and went inside the house.

"She doesn't sleep," said Julia's father. "She talks non-stop. She's raking up things that happened years ago."

"How long has she been like this?"

"A week . . . ten days. She won't rest. I can't get anything done." His tone was exasperated. Julia was sitting on the bottom step of the stairs. The front door was wide open so she could still see her mother. Julia was hurt by her father's disloyalty. Why was he complaining to Dr Stuart?

"You should have contacted me earlier. Can I use your phone?" The doctor made a call to the psychiatric ward at the local hospital. It was the ward where Julia's mother had worked before she was married. Ward 17. Her father used to phone her mother there to ask her out to dances.

"It's Dr Stuart, I'm with a Mrs Fell. No previous admissions." He made a stab at a diagnosis. "Paranoid schizophrenia." When Julia heard these words, they entered her body and ricocheted like a pinball flipping against the four walls of a glass case. He put the phone down. "There's a bed waiting for her. You can take her, or I can call an ambulance."

"Does she have to go? Can't we look after her here?" Julia's father asked.

"I'm sorry, Mr Fell. It's gone too far for that."

"I'll take her," said her father. Julia was relieved. She couldn't bear the thought of an ambulance coming up the road to take her mother away.

The three of them persuaded Julia's mother to come inside. She took her place on the settee. "You need looking after for a while, Mrs Fell. It won't be for long." Julia wanted to believe him.

"I want to hear *What a Wonderful World*. Satchmo. He's my favourite," said Julia's mother.

"I'll leave you to it, Mr Fell. The hospital will keep me informed." Julia opened the front door for him. She wanted to stay as long as possible with this person who seemed to understand what was going on.

Her father slid the record down the rod in the middle of the radiogram deck and lifted the arm across. The speakers clicked when the needle hit the vinyl.

I see trees of green, red roses too,
I see them bloom for me and you . . .

The three of them sat on the lilac three-piece suite. Julia darted looks at her mother, then at her father.

The colours of the rainbow, so pretty in the sky . . .

Her mother was staring out of the window, at the crab apple tree. The blossom was damp and heavy with rain. A single gust of wind sent a shower of petals spinning past the window. The record came to an end and the player clicked off.

"I want to hear it again," said Julia's mother.

"We've got to go, love," said her father.

"I want to hear it again," said her mother. There was something in her tone—a determined insistence, which made Julia's father replace the arm on the disk. They all sat and listened again. Julia's mother stroked the back of her hand—three times on the left and four times on the right. She joined in with the end of each line of the song. Julia was glad when it reached its final refrain.

And I think to myself, what a wonderful world,
Yes, I think to myself, what a wonderful world.

The player clicked off again.

"One more time," said Julia's mother.

"Mum, it's time to go," pleaded Julia.

"After this," said her mother. "I'll go after this time." Julia set the arm on the disk. She stood next to the gram, ready to leave, looking at the family photograph on the sideboard. They were picking blackberries in Redisher Woods. Her mother was holding up her juice-stained hands to the camera. Julia was brandishing a walking stick. Blackberry picking was something they did every year, in anticipation of pies and jam. Julia could almost feel the grit of the seeds in her mouth. When the last note of the song had finished, Julia switched off the gram. Her father held out his hand to her mother.

The following Monday Julia arrived at school late and tearful. She'd missed assembly and was hoping to slip into her classroom unseen. The building smelled of sawdust and disinfectant. A girl from her class was making her way down the same staircase. "Are you alright?" she asked. It was Pamela Bell. They weren't particular friends, but Julia respected Pamela. She seemed mature and worldly to Julia. In fact it was Pamela that Julia voted for as head girl six years later.

"My mum's mentally ill."

"What's wrong with her?"

"She's having a nervous breakdown."

"A nervous breakdown isn't a mental illness," said Pamela. "She'll be OK." Pamela seemed to know what she was talking about and Julia felt comforted. They both went into the classroom, just as their Latin teacher arrived.

On her way home, Julia climbed the stone steps into the

public library. She walked around the shelves looking at the classifications—Natural History, Cookery, Philosophy. She knew that she needed psychiatry, that psychology explained what was wrong and that psychiatry cured it. There, on the top shelf under the high window, was the word PSYCHIATRY printed in black letters and laminated onto yellow card. She ran her fingers along the titles. *Psychiatry and Anti-Psychiatry*, *Six Lectures on Psychoanalytic Psychiatry*, *The New Language of Psychiatry*. She took the last book down off the shelf and looked at the contents page. Did her mother have a neurosis or a psychosis? Julia didn't know. The book was complicated and technical. She replaced it in the gap on the shelf. Maybe she should study these subjects at university instead of the English degree she had planned.

It was lonely when Julia came home from school. Her mother had always been there to greet her. They would eat together, exchanging the odd word. Sometimes Julia would read at the table. She knew she shouldn't, but her mother never asked her not to, and she was always keen to finish the book. Her father was often late home and he would eat alone, waited on by her mother. Now, when her father came home, he was invariably in a sour mood.

"What is this doing here?" he snapped, picking up some object which wasn't in its usual place. Julia would be cut to the quick. There was so much to worry about, she couldn't understand why he got so angry about such small things. One evening, as they sat together in the sitting room, he talked to her in a way he never had before. "I should never have married your mother," he said. "I had plenty of girlfriends. I should have married Olwyn. She was a farm girl. Rosy cheeks and always smiling." Julia squirmed. She didn't want to hear that he could have been happier with someone else.

Most days he would visit the hospital. Usually Julia went with him. For the first few days her mother railed at her father. "Why did you put me here? I want to go home. I want to go home!" Julia would stand behind her mother's chair with her hand on her shoulder. She couldn't sit between her parents and listen to her mother. The room was thick with cigarette smoke. Some patients sat in chairs, staring; some went about their business; and some stood or hovered, uncertain, like models about to adopt a pose. Julia remembered that her mother had worked on this ward. In the school holidays the two of them would sit down for dinner.

"Tell me a story about when you were a nurse," Julia would ask. Her mother would pause, then begin.

"I wore a dress with stripes. With a white starched apron and a cap. The doors of the ward were always locked in those days. Each nurse had a key. The sick ward wasn't supposed to be left unattended. But one day it was very hot and the side door was open. I was alone doing the dressing trolley. A patient ran out into the garden wearing only an open back nightdress. I ran after her. She stopped and put her arms round a tree. What a sight, poor soul. I helped her back to the ward. Then I was pulled over the coals by Sister for leaving the ward."

As the days went on, Julia's mother seemed more settled. She got to know the other patients. She enjoyed more company on the ward than she did off it. "I know all their stories," she said. She was an exceptional listener.

After her ECT treatments she'd be ashen and withdrawn. One Saturday afternoon there was blood on her cardigan. Her ear was ripped. "They pulled my earring. Yanked it out," she said, angrily, putting her lobe between her finger and thumb. "See? They split my ear." Julia was horrified. On the way out they looked for a member of staff.

"She was trying to escape," the nurse said, as though it was perfectly normal. Julia had never known her mother behave badly. "It was the fifth time this morning. I went to grab her and my hand caught her earring." It sounded perfectly feasible, but Julia didn't know what to believe. What if there was no end to the brutality of the staff after the visitors had left?

Six weeks after she'd been admitted, Julia's mother was ready to go home. On Julia's last visit she accompanied her and her father down the stairs to the exit door. She looked at the flower beds which lined the path up to the entrance.

"The roses are out. Pink and red all in a line. Can you see that room over there?" she pointed across the hallway. "That's where I was given a party when I got married. All the staff came from Ward 17. *And* matron. They bought me a bedding box. The Lloyd Loom one in the bathroom. I painted it yellow."

Julia and her father cleaned the house from top to bottom and shopped for everything they could think of. Julia waited at home while her father went to collect her mother. She paced up and down in the front room, trying not to look out of the window too often. To distract herself, she picked out one of the thick heavy seventy-eight records which were stacked side by side in the radiogram. She made herself read every word on the middle of the disk. *Dvorak's Humoreske, Opus 101, Number 7. Liberal Jewish Synagogue Organ, St. John's Wood, London.* The heaving organ began, but there was a bad scratch across the disk—Julia tried to ignore it. Halfway through the piece the car drew up outside. Julia ran to the door.

She put her arms round her mother and realized how thin she'd become. The drugs and the ECT had wrung her out. She was quiet, and when she did speak, her voice was flat and empty of its usual warmth. Her face was still. Over the next few days she took her medication and slowly picked up her chores—wiping dust from the leaves of the castor oil plant, stirring her soup on the electric cooker, wiping down the Formica surfaces in the kitchen.

When Julia packed her bag to go to Janice's, she put her troll on top of her clothes. Janice had a troll too. They spent hours combing their hair—stroking it, backcombing, plaiting, and tying it up in ribbons. Their trolls stood together on Janice's dressing table while Julia was getting ready for the birthday party. She tried to block out any thoughts of home. It was a relief to be in a household where everyone behaved how you'd expect them to.

The birthday buffet spilled over the dining room table—cheese and pineapple on sticks, pink cocktail sausages, bridge rolls with four different fillings, fairy cakes in paper cases and a white-iced Victoria sponge with birthday wishes piped in pink. When most of it was eaten, everyone was asked to congregate in the front room for a game. Janice's parents had arranged a line of objects in the middle of the carpet—a silver candelabra, a tall cut glass vase, a transistor radio, a newspaper rack, a table lamp, a wastepaper bin and a pot of pink lilies. Janice's father explained the game.

"I'll take one of you at a time and the rest can wait in the dining room for their turn. You'll be blindfolded and then it's my job to guide you. You have to step over the objects without knocking them over—or even touching them. If you touch them then you're out. Janice—it's your birthday, you go first. And if everyone else can wait in the dining room, please." Julia went next door to wait for her turn. Janice's mother was emptying the table into the kitchen. There were crumbs and cocktails sticks scattered across the carpet.

After a while, Julia heard a yelp from the front room and then prolonged whispering. "Julia, your turn now!" called Janice. She went through and turned around so that Janice could blindfold her. Janice's father took her hand.

"We'll go over here to the start of the line. That's right." he said. "Now, step forward just a little bit more. Now lift your leg. Bit higher, just a bit more . . . that's it. Put it down. Now bring the other leg up. Down you go. That's it, splendid! Now it's the glass vase, so we don't want to knock that over, do we? Higher, bit higher. That's it! Well done! The transistor now—so small step. Easy peasy." He went on like this till she got to the end of the line. "Now the lilies. Last thing. We don't want soil all over the carpet, so try your hardest. Higher . . . high as you can . . . bit higher. That's it, terrific! You've done it!"

Julia pulled the scarf from her eyes and slid it over her chin. She turned round to check that all the objects were still standing. But there was nothing there. The carpet was empty. Even before she'd taken her first step, the objects had been removed.

CREATIVE LIGHTING

IT WAS THIS PART which Mia couldn't get used to—standing between the two locked and sealed doors. For a few seconds she was trapped. There was a time lapse after one door closed and before the other one opened. She had to remind herself that this was just a faint echo of the incarceration of the five hundred men inside. Sure, they'd committed some very serious crimes, the nature of which for the most part Mia was unaware, but their total loss of liberty was not something she could imagine. Her boss had asked to be locked in a cell for half an hour as part of her training, but what was that compared to thirty years?

Mia had keys to all of the doors which led to the Education Block. She wore them in a black leather peggy purse strapped diagonally across her torso. This was her fifth month teaching creative writing, mornings and afternoons on a Thursday, at HMP Belmarsh. She'd seen the snowdrops and hyacinth in the meagre flowerbeds change to the current regiments of vermilion geraniums. Winter and summer, the men hung washing out of their windows—loops of jeans and T-shirts, trainers tied together, and the occasional sarong. Usually they shouted or whistled at her as she walked alongside the tall, featureless, red-brick blocks. She would wave or, on a good day, curtsey.

So far her classes had gone well. She'd never had call to press the red alarm button in her teaching room; the men seemed to enjoy her sessions. They liked the camaraderie—so rather than setting individual tasks, Mia devised an activity for each session which involved some kind of discussion. Anyone who couldn't write would tell a story. The older guys invariably finished up advising the younger guys on how to survive their sentence.

The men could choose in the day between education, work, and staying in their cells. When they selected a subject from the curriculum, some picked on the words 'creative writing' without really knowing what they meant.

One guy arrived first to a session and asked, "Do you provide the pens?"

"Yes," she answered, handing him a blue biro.

"I thought they were ink pens. You know, with a flat end on the nib," the man said.

Mia paused and asked, "What class did you sign up for?"

"Fancy writing . . . beginning with 'C'. What do you call it?"

"Creative?" offered Mia.

"No. What is it? . . . Calligraphy."

Another man came in and sat on the only empty chair. "Will we do practical stuff," he asked, "like fixing spots and mixing colours and that?"

"What class are you looking for?" asked Mia.

"Creative Lighting," said the guy, straight-faced.

The men were late coming down from the wings that day. There was often a security alert or an incident which would prevent the smooth flow of the timetable. Mia had laid out her stash of anthologies and literary magazines; she'd arranged the cream roses from her garden in a large plastic beaker; she'd put up a couple of posters of 'Poems on the Underground' with Sellotape. She knew the posters would be adopted by the men and taken back to their cells, but at least they would be read and enjoyed. Mia had originally used Blu Tack to attach posters to the peppermint walls, until a de-briefing session when her boss spoke to her rather sharply, "Mia, have you ever thought what Blu Tack could be used for?"

"Sorry?" said Mia.

"Other than attaching posters to the wall?"

"Pretend chewing gum?" suggested Mia.

"You press a key into it and get a cast made." Mia put her hand over her open mouth.

Now she could hear movement along the corridors. Men

started to file down the stairs and filter into the rooms around the atrium. Art was to her left, politics to her right. "Hello, Miss," said a beaming Turkish guy, Omah.

"Good morning, Mia," said a pale Albanian, Lucash.

"Hi, there," said Midge, a dishevelled Lancastrian.

Some were silent and nodded; others didn't make eye contact but sat themselves down and stared out of the window at the wall opposite, crowned with coils of razor wire. Mia had photocopied two poems for them to look at. Some of the men had started to read them, some needed to be encouraged. "You'll see that both poems are quite long, and each line in each poem begins with the word 'For.' *My Cat Jeoffry* was written by Christopher Smart in 1760. *My Lover* is by Wendy Cope and she published her first collection of poems in 1986."

"Big difference," said Omah.

"Absolutely. Would anyone like to have a bash at reading the Christopher Smart?" Omah half-raised his hand. Just as he drew breath, another face appeared round the door.

"Creative Writing?" asked a short-haired man with a cheeky face. Mia nodded.

"I'm Jeffrey," he said, with boundless confidence.

"Come and join us," said Mia. He took the only empty seat and adjusted his glasses as he looked down at the copies of the two poems. Mia nodded to Omah to begin. He read the whole poem straight through.

"I thought you could pick out your favourite lines and underline them. Don't worry if there are some lines you don't understand, just pick the ones you like." Mia looked at the top of their heads as they scrutinized the poem. Some were shaved, some were scarred, some were tattooed. After a few minutes, Mia asked Midge to read the lines he'd chosen. He read with a faltering, flat, slightly accusatory tone.

"For I will consider my Cat Jeoffrey. . .
For he is of the tribe of Tiger. . .
For every family had one cat at least in the bag.
For the English Cats are the best in Europe. . .
For he is the quickest to his mark of any creature. . .
Poor Jeoffrey! Poor Jeoffry! the rat has bit thy throat . . ."

At the end of every couple of lines, Midge shot a glance

round the room. Jeffrey maintained a practised grin on his face throughout.

"For, though he cannot fly, he is an excellent
clamberer. . .
For he can swim for life.
For he can creep."

"Thank you, Midge. Jeffrey, would you like to read the Wendy Cope? You'll see that she has borrowed Christopher Smart's structure—again, each line begins with 'For', but her poem has a much more contemporary feel."

"Of course," said Jeffrey. He cleared his throat.

"My Lover
For I will consider my lover, who shall remain
nameless.
For at the age of 49 he can make the noise of five different kinds
of lorry changing gear on a hill.
For he sometimes does this on the stairs at his place of work."

He read as though he were giving a sermon in a church.

"For he is obsessed with sex.
For he would never say it is overrated."

Everyone looked serious.

"For when I asked if this necklace is alright he replies,
'Yes, if it means looking at three others."

He slowed down towards the end to gain maximum effect.

"Thank you, Jeffrey. Lovely. What I'd like you to have a go at is writing your own version of the Wendy Cope. Begin each line with 'For'. Can anyone give me a line?" Mia got up to stand by the board to write down suggestions. "Perhaps if we all begin, 'For I will consider my lover, who shall remain nameless.'"

George, a teenage Afro-Caribbean boy, spoke first. "For she is real fit, and I never get tired of her, if you know what I mean." He rolled his eyes at his mates. There was the first laughter of the morning.

"I've got one, Miss . . . Mia," said Midge. "'For she brings me a nice cuppa tea in the morning'. How good would that be?" Mia scribed onto the board.

"Lucash?" His hand was waving in the air.

"For she gave me three beautiful children." Mia wrote down his words.

"Lovely. You've got it," she told Lucash. "You don't need me anymore."

"I've got one for our Jeffrey," said Midge.

"Well, I'm sure Jeffrey's got enough of his own, Midge," said Mia.

"How about, 'For she stood by me through thick and thin. Silly cow.'" A snigger went up. Jeffrey put on his useful grin.

"Or, 'For she makes a mean shepherd's pie,'" said Omah. Jeffrey looked as though he was about to say something, but then thought better of it.

"OK, guys," said Mia, "I think we've got enough now to be able to start."

Mia was grateful when the buzzer sounded for association. She wasn't sure how much longer she could hold it together. The men filed out in twos and threes. "For you are an arsehole and you should be banned from the face of the earth," said Omah to Midge. Midge laughed. He was about to sink into one of the comfy chairs outside, but instead he strolled back into Mia's room.

"Watch yourself, Miss. Don't let him give you any money. And you'd better start keeping a diary." She allowed herself a half smile.

That evening Mia took a knife to a red pepper and slit it so it splayed in half. She spread it on her marble chopping board, pulled at the pith and the seeds, and sliced the red juicy flesh into strips. "I couldn't believe it when he walked in."

"But you knew he was in the prison?" said Bill, her Glaswegian boyfriend.

"Of course. But I never thought Jeffrey Archer would come to my class."

"What happened in the second half?"

"I got them writing again and redrafting. Then we read out."

"What was his like?"

"Awful—full of clichés. 'For she walks with me in these cool corridors. For I see her in my mind's eye deadheading the roses. For her voice sends me into raptures. For there is more wisdom in her little finger than in the minds of a thousand leaders.'"

"Oh yeah!" Bill added his own line. "For she is very fragrant, but has entirely lost her sense of smell."

He handed Mia a glass of chilled wine.

"Well, he won't be drinking Australian Chardonnay tonight," he said.

"The guys were asking him about bestsellers. How do you write one? One of them suggested he started 'bestseller classes' on the wing."

Bill broke four eggs into a bowl and began to beat them with a balloon whisk. "Will he?"

"I doubt it." Mia watched Bill pour the eggs into the pan of sizzling butter. She looked at the line of his mouth—how it rose to the promontory of his cupid's bow, then fell to the smile line at the corner of his mouth.

When they sat on their patio with their omelettes on their knees, Mia looked at the lines of their garden—the curves they had cut into the grass, the lengths of bamboo supporting a crown of cerise sweet peas, the trunk of the winter flowering cherry which grew thicker and more glossy every year. Here was her satisfaction. She did not crave wealth, fame, power or celebrity. Her contentment came from the way Bill would touch the end of her nose with his finger, for no apparent reason, or from a day spent in the North Sea being buffeted by vigorous waves.

There was one particular beach they liked to visit on the coast of Suffolk. The sand cliffs were punctured with a line of holes where swifts nested. There were bleached grey limbs from trees which had toppled from the fields above. Bill and Mia would stretch out the length of a day—lounging, swimming, wandering to the lagoon to watch the terns.

They could even make love if it was a quiet weekday. Bill would inch towards her on his elbows and pull a towel over them. Just as Mia was about to come, Bill often asked, "Who are you thinking of?" Mia's reply was always the same. "Only of you," she said as she struggled to banish the register of faces from her mind—Midge, Omah, George, Lucash.

Each time they drove back into London, Mia was more acutely aware of the shrinking vistas. Instead of a cruise ship or a flat oil tanker skimming the line where the sea met the sky, high rise flats, flyovers and endless roundabouts pushed into her fore-ground. When she was back home, the garden became her land-scape, a watercolour in the bathroom of a boat tilted on Dunwich beach became her way back to the sea.

Mia over-prepared her prison session for the following Thursday. She wanted to avoid any possible conflict. She covered the rectangle of tables in her room with poems and photographs and postcards. Her tape recorder was ready with an early recording of Dylan Thomas. She even devised a literary quiz, carefully based on work they had already done.

Most of the men arrived early that day. It was always impossible to predict. Many looked tired and drawn, as though they hadn't slept properly in weeks.

"Can I have this book?" asked Omah, picking up a twentieth century anthology of short stories.

"You can borrow it, if you promise to bring it back next week," said Mia.

"OK."

She got him to sign a piece of paper. The men began to pick up the postcards and turn them over to see what was written on the back. Just then Jeffrey appeared at the door.

"I'm sorry," he said smiling broadly, "I won't be joining you this week. Or any other week, I'm afraid. I've changed to Media Studies. Creative Writing isn't really for me." Mia nodded and addressed her class.

SAND SHIFT

DOROTHY WAS WAKING UP. Trains were pulling out of the station below. Announcements warned and informed. She remembered again that she was alone. Snatches of sleep had provided rare respite. Watery sunlight filtered the rose-patterned curtains and picked out the meagre furniture pushed up against the walls. She closed her eyes again, not wanting the day to come any closer. She didn't believe in the space beside her. "Is the kettle on, Dot?" he would say, knowing full well that it wasn't. Then there would begin the gentle cajoling of the day into breakfast.

She tried to sleep again, but the day had already intruded too far. She pulled herself up on her pillow. Her joints ached with fatigue and the wear and tear of six decades. Breakfast in bed? That was only allowed on Sundays, and birthdays, of course. And anniversaries and illness. They'd neither of then had much illness. The usual bouts of flu, even minor operations, but nothing long and drawn out.

She folded back the sheets and blankets and put her feet into her waiting slippers. They'd never gone in for duvets. They liked the daily routine of folding the covers, lifting over the counterpane, smoothing the valance. When the air was caught under the sheet, Bill would say it was like a tent, or a parachute. The tray was ready in the kitchen. Teabags in the pot, two cups and saucers, two plates. Bill had had the veto on loose tea, which Dorothy did prefer. But for the sake of the stainless steel sink and occasional blockages, she had relented.

When the tea was brewed and the plates filled with white bread toast, butter and blackcurrant jam, she went back to bed and felt guilty. She poured two cups of tea, drank one, and ate one plate of toast. Without giving herself a moment for digestion, she returned the tray to the kitchen and shuffled hastily into the bathroom. The bathroom didn't have a window. It did have a red pull string. If there was any problem, a pull of the string would set off flashing lights in the corridor. The flats had been built with older tenants in mind. All the light switches were at waist level.

But the light switch in the bathroom was faulty. Dorothy fumbled around in the natural light from the doorway and trod on a towel which had slipped from its rail. A primeval moan gathered in her lungs and hung in her throat. Four months ago she had come home to find Bill arranged over the bathroom floor. He lay face down, knees bent, with his arms folded underneath his chest. His slippers had fallen off his feet. Before pulling the red cord, Dorothy had knelt and replaced the slippers on his stocking feet. The memory ricocheted—her neighbour making the phone call, the alarming siren of the ambulance, the sombre doctor mouthing his litany. "Would have been sudden. Over very quickly. He wouldn't have felt much pain." She felt absented, without any part to play. It was out of her hands.

Dorothy bent to replace the towel, straightened up without having picked it up and wandered into the living room. She sat in the middle of the sofa, rested her head on the arm, clutched a cushion to her stomach and drew up her knees. She could hear the starlings and sparrows pecking into the peanuts on the balcony. The trains pulled in relentlessly at twenty-minute intervals and the pendulum in the domed clock swung out its irrelevant rhythm.

After a rally of arrivals and departures, Dorothy roused herself and trailed back into the bedroom to put on yesterday's clothes. In fact, she'd been wearing the mint green, button-through jumper since the weekend. Bill had rarely commented or complimented her on her appearance, but for some reason he had picked out this particular jumper. She walked along the short narrow corridor to the short narrow galley kitchen. The flat was compact, economical on space and identical to the other three flats on the same floor. The door to each flat opened onto a communal corridor. Each resident marked the approach to their door with pieces of carpet, potted plants and pictures. Dorothy had hung a souvenir from their Portuguese holiday— two white ceramic villas, each with window boxes, geraniums and red tiles.

After Bill retired, they went each day to the park to feed the birds. They would kid each other into buying far more bread than they needed to make sure of their supplies. Now Dorothy had to scavenge in the empty bread tin. She retrieved the uneaten toast from the overflowing pedal bin. The bread barely weighted down the flimsy carrier bag. She put on her raincoat without checking the weather and went out into the lift. There were two lifts, one considerably longer than the other. They had christened this the coffin lift. They would gamble on which lift would arrive. If it was the coffin lift, they would challenge it to cast a slight on the day. Today the smaller lift arrived.

The air was mild for November, but the clench of an early cold snap had brought premature leaves to the ground. Dorothy's head was bowed as she walked, one hand thrust deep in her pocket, her fingers sifting seaside pebbles and train tickets.

The park was quiet of people—schools not yet out, dog walkers mostly away to work. Dorothy cut her usual path up the central hill to the gated terraced garden. Winter flowering shrubs sang staccato amidst the bare black trees. The grey squirrels, confused by the mildness, continued to dart wary looks and gather clutches of sweet chestnuts for the colder months.

Dorothy put her bag on a wooden bench. It bore a tiny plaque to an erstwhile spouse. She filled her fists with crumbs and stretched her arms out in front of her. Feathers fluttered round her face and eager beaks nipped her palms. A woman and child stood and watched. One of the gardeners waved over in recognition. The bread soon ran out. The birds flew off, the woman and child carried on their walk, and the gardener went back to his digging.

Dorothy sat back on the bench. The billow of her coat sent the carrier bag to the ground. She looked ahead but saw nothing of the landscaped hummocks, church spires, towers and terraced houses teaming towards the horizon. The trains were distant now. The church clock struck the quarter hours. The afternoon grew into chill. Dorothy leaned forward, pulled her coat around her and gripped her knees together. She hugged herself hard, but her body had no warmth to kindle. The light was weakening, her eyes focused on the foreground.

Nestling next to a blank flowerbed she could see a tiny blue glove, knitted round with ducks and geese. She picked it up and studied its brightness in her shallow palm. She remembered her grandson having a similar glove. Mark was four now. He was in Australia with her daughter and son-in-law. They had emigrated three years ago. Dorothy had been asked if she would like to join them, to live with them permanently, but she wasn't ready to leave. She wanted to stay in contact with the places which would prompt and feed her memories.

She put the glove in her pocket and started for home by way of the boating lake. The lake was empty now, it made a sunken platform for skateboards and rollerblades. On through the children's park, a solitary woman was pushing her son in a boxed-in swing. Dorothy stopped. It was the two who had watched her feeding the birds. She wondered about the glove. The little boy wasn't wearing any. She held back, loathe to approach a stranger.

She hadn't spoken to anyone for days. She wasn't sure if she would be able to say what was necessary. But the woman looked friendly enough, and the thought of the little boy having one useless odd glove spurred her on. She held out the glove. "Sorry. I saw you earlier. Is this yours?"

"Yes! Oh, thank you. I didn't think we'd find it. Tim, look, this lady has found your glove. Say thank you." Tim turned in his swing and smiled with gratitude, then wanted to be pushed some more.

"They're so demanding at this age. He's four. Ready for school really. Itching to go."

The woman talked with ease. Dorothy didn't have to say much, just interjected with the occasional encouraging murmur. 'She must be glad of a little adult company,' Dorothy thought. When she could no longer bear her own silence she said, "Well I must be getting back." She felt awkward, but the words came out reasonably well.

"Maybe we'll bump into you again. We're usually here around this time."

"Yes."

"I'm Sheila."

Dorothy offered her name and retreated.

As she walked out of the gates she mulled over the meeting. Despite her discomfort, she had enjoyed listening to Sheila talk about her recent move to the area from the North. How difficult it was to start over again. How she never thought she would get used to the city. Dorothy liked her openness and her calm manner with Tim. Tim was similar only in age to Mark. Mark was very fair, bleached and tanned. Tim was dark with an indoor complexion.

By the time Dorothy arrived home it was quite dark. She stood a while at the window before pulling the curtains. The lights from the opposite flats cut luminous boxes into the night. She went into the kitchen to make some tea, setting the tray with two cups, two saucers and an art deco milk jug gleaned from the local flea market. The kettle came to the boil, she poured the water into the warmed pot. Before taking the tray into the living room she returned the second cup and saucer to the cupboard.

BATES GREEN

As I spooned the juice over the no-longer-dried peaches and pears, I could hear Will sweet-talking the other two guests. "So, you're here to do some serious walking?" His enthusiasm for strangers was never feigned, but I often wondered if he would have any left in reserve for me.

"We're leaving the car here and getting trains and buses along the way," said Laura, a newly-wed from Godalming.

Her husband, Greg, continued, "Lunch at the Rose Cottage Inn at Alciston, then evening meal at the Ram Inn at Firle. Not that food marks our every choice of route!"

Laura giggled. I went to sit down with my dish of compôte and organic natural yoghurt. "Oh, you've got compôtée too," said Laura. Her husband didn't correct her pronunciation, and neither did we. "I liked it so much when we came before that I made some for my family, at Christmas. 'Here, have some compôtée.' Nobody wanted any. Must have been something wrong."

"You've been here before?" I asked.

"Last year," Greg and Laura said at the same time.

"It was during the foot-and-mouth, so we couldn't walk," said Greg.

"But it was so lovely we wanted to come again," said Laura.

"It *is* lovely," I agreed.

"Have you been in the woods?" asked Will.

"No," said Greg. Laura shook her head.

"They're sublime, aren't they Sam?" Will's eyes were wide as he looked at me for a response. I nodded. "If you go while the sun is still out you can see millions, literally millions of white anemones with their faces open. It is *stunning*. If the light catches them in a certain way it can look as though the woods are flooded." I loved to hear Will describe experiences we had just had; it stretched them further out into the world.

Greg looked at Laura. "That sounds a must," said Laura.

"After that write-up we can't miss it," said Greg,

In the middle of the breakfast table there was a posy of flowers in a small porcelain jug—marsh marigolds, narcissus, pulminaria and grape hyacinth. The scent from the narcissus drifted towards me. "Oh, that's wonderful," I said, picking up the vase and pushing my nose against the yolk yellow petals.

"We've got a vase of flowers like that in our room," said Laura, "but they're plastic."

"Are you sure?" I asked. "They do look as though they might be plastic, but I bet if you touch them . . . We've got the same in our room, same smell."

"I'll take a closer look when we go up," said Laura, her young face eager with a smile.

"*You* won't get invited back," joked Will, his fair fringe dancing in front of his eyes.

It seemed in that moment that nothing would ever change. That Greg and Laura would go on making plans to walk long distance footpaths with stops for meals at reputable pubs, that there would always be time for compôte and sausages and fresh coffee for breakfast, and that conviviality over a meal with strangers was something to be taken for granted.

Will made to pour me another cup of coffee. I put my hand over my cup.

"We must make a move," said Greg.

"Let's all get up together," I suggested. We all stood up and replaced our chairs neatly under the table.

"Have a good walk," said Will. "And take care. We don't want to hear reports of you falling the length of the Old Man of Wilmington!"

"That would be a poor effort," said Greg as he climbed the stairs.

"See you on some headland or other," I said as we parted on the landing.

Bates Green is a bed and breakfast place for 'garden lovers'. It hadn't been difficult to pick this property from the guidebook. *An eighteenth century tile-hung farmhouse with a well-established garden—mixed borders, a pond, a formal garden and two meadows.* It seemed the obvious choice for a belated wedding anniversary treat. I lifted the heavy wooden latch and pushed open the door to our room.

"Weren't they sweet?" I said, falling onto my unmade bed.

"Very," said Will.

I'd been glad that there was only the twin room left when Will had booked. Just a sliver of space between the two beds. Just a little more choice about whether or not to be skin-close. In the seventeen years we'd been together we never stopped wanting each other. Will's son didn't live with us, so there was always time to dip into bed in the afternoon, or lie-in long in the mornings.

So why did I need Neil? Why did I, week after week, deceive Will without a second thought? He was so *easy* to deceive. Not that that made me think any less of him.

"I'm staying at Gill's tonight. We're going to have a drink, so I don't want to drive back."

"I'll see you tomorrow evening then, love." His smile was long and easy.

It was the anticipation I enjoyed the most. Seeing Neil's name in my inbox— that special configuration of numbers and letters. The way the layers of possible meaning in his message peeled away through the day.

The first time I ever saw him was in the corridor. Our eyes caught between Environmental Health and Housing. His hair had insistent dark curls and he always wore snazzy ties. After a couple of weeks of smiles we were introduced in the The Malted Shovel—the nearest pub for Greenwich council employees to fall into after a day's work. It was dark and dingy, and Neilson was forever singing on the jukebox about not being able to live without me.

"So, what's it like working in Housing?" Neil asked.

"Probably as fascinating as looking after dustbins."

"Master of the drains, that's me."

"Are you married?" I asked, spotting the ring on his left hand.

"Twelve years and two children."

"What does your wife do?"

"Lies in bed all day."

"Oh!"

"Not what you might think. She's ill. Some kind of unspecified chronic thing."

Maybe I felt sorry for him.

"I used to be a rock star," Neil said the second time we came across each other in the pub. Everyone else had gone. We were the only ones left sitting on the maroon banquette.

"Yeah, right."

"It's true. I played bass in a band. The Geysers. We were really hot." I laughed. "We could have had a record contract. If we'd been in the right place at the right time."

Van Morrison was singing *Brown Eyed Girl* on the jukebox.

"Were you as good as that?" I asked.

"Maybe not."

We would book a hotel for the night and take it in turns to pay. The Hilton Dartford Bridge was our favourite—far enough away for us not to bump into anyone we knew, and just the right mix of neo-thirties-brutalist architecture and motorway service station-lack-of-chic. Its greatest claim was its proximity to Bluewater shopping centre.

I'd meet Neil in the Court Bar. He'd usually be there when I arrived. I'd order a gin and tonic and go and sit beside him.

"What took you so long?"

"I drove as fast as I could."

"Come off it. You never go above seventy."

"Some of us are law-abiding citizens."

"When it pleases you."

"So, you're wearing the blue silk tie today."

"Thought it was a blue silk sort-of-a-day."

"What does that mean?"

Mostly I listened. He'd talk about his old music friends, his under-achieving children and the latest staff machinations at the council. Then we'd go upstairs to our room. The bedcover always had the same huge floral design with orange roses or blue hydrangeas, and the smell of over-sweet air freshener hung in the middle of the room. If we were hungry we'd phone room service. Neil called once at three o'clock in the morning. "I'd like two fillet steaks, rare, with fries, and two knickerbocker glories." It arrived on a trolley half an hour later, the steaks hidden under great silver domes. We didn't eat most of it. The pink ice cream ran down the side of the tall glasses, hiding the fruit and red jelly.

On our third night together he produced a plastic bag of white powder from his pocket and gave me a silent smile. He tipped out some of the powder onto the glass-topped coffee table, made two stripes with his credit card, and gestured to me. "You go."

"No, you first," I said. I'd never taken cocaine before and I wanted to watch what he did. I bent forward and sniffed gently so that my breath lasted for its length. Later that night, as we were sitting up in bed, he poured the white powder along the length of his penis. "What am I supposed to do with that?"

"What do you think?"

It wasn't as if the sex was anything special. It was rushed and cursory. Will, on the other hand, was considerate and he took his time. But that didn't seem to be the point. I needed to be something other than a wife, a sister, a manager, a dutiful daughter.

I'd get home afterwards and turn the key in the door. Our old black cat always greeted me. I'd carry her from room to room looking at the our accumulated possessions — the carefully chosen furniture, the collection of etched glasses, the prints of American landscapes hanging in the hall; and the photographs of our dead fathers, our adolescent nephews and our contented friends, which stood in ranks on the display cabinet.

I looked at myself in the unfamiliar bathroom mirror. My eyes looked back at me, but they didn't have any answers. The door was open and I could see Will sitting on the bed leafing through an old copy of *Good Housekeeping* he'd found by his bedside. "Did you know that mosquitoes don't like the smell of basil?" he said. "We'll have to keep a pot by the bed. I want to be the only thing that bites you."

I went over to him, put my arm around his shoulder and

nursed his head into my belly. If ever I was going to tell him about Neil it would have to be now—with the spring light streaming over the pillows and the cups from our morning tea carefully stacked on the tray. I started to cry. "What is it?" asked Will. I cried tears for another man into the back of Will's downy neck.

The next morning at breakfast we were alone. Greg and Lara had already eaten. "This was the perfect choice," said Will. "The view from the Downs over those patterned hills to the sea—hmm."

"I'm glad," I said. "I wanted you to enjoy it."

"And you needed a break. You mustn't let work get to you like that, love."

"No. You're right." He put his hand over my hand and teased a strand of hair away from my eyes. I smiled at him.

Car doors were slamming outside. Greg and Lara were throwing rucksacks into their Ford Fiesta. "Don't speak to me like that!" Lara shouted at Greg. Greg put his hand on Lara's arm. She pushed it away and grabbed the car keys from his hand. Doors slammed again. Lara revved the engine and the tyres skidded on the gravel driveway as she turned towards the road. Will and I looked at each other in disbelief.

After that weekend I decided not to see Neil again. Whenever an email came from him I deleted it straight away. I tried not to think for the rest of the day what it might have said. Gradually it became easier. I thought of him less and less. He became a dulled presence in my memory. If he appeared in my mind—laughing or raising an eyebrow—I told myself he was someone I used to know.

Three months went by. Will and I made plans to build a conservatory. We booked a holiday in New York. I stopped expecting to hear from Neil.

I was choosing between tortellini and ravioli for supper in Sainsbury's when my phone rang. "Hi, there. How's it going?" he asked.

"Neil?"

"Yeah. Who else? How've you been?"

"Alright."

"It's been ages. I've been missing you. Look, I can't talk now, I'm driving, but it'd be great to see you. Can we meet? Tomorrow? Thursday?"

"Tomorrow would be good."

"Shall I book?"

"Why not?" I picked up two packs of tortellini and made my way to the checkout.

JAMES STEWART WAS MY UNCLE CHARLIE

CHARLIE WAS TALL. HE had the grace and dignity of a galleon. He made me feel as though I was the only person in the world. The last time I saw him was in a nursing home in St. Anne's. That bitter October I phoned the home to ask for directions. The woman in charge said, "It's a pink thing, stands back from the road. St. Andrew's Road South." Charlie was staying there while he waited for his 'prostrate' operation. He'd had the operation once but it had grown back again.

He'd already had a hip replacement, for which he'd waited two years. He could have gone private for £5,000, but he didn't, on principal. "After all that money I've paid in over the years," he said. "And I don't want to jump the queue in front of some little old lady."

After his first prostate operation he stood in the doorway of the men's surgical ward with a colostomy bag hanging from the waist of his pyjamas. A fellow patient stood in the opposite doorway, pointing at the bag. "Charlie," he shouts, "your goldfish is dead!"

I took down the directions to the nursing home—after the church, over the bridge and then second on the left. She seemed to know it was Charlie I would be visiting even before I said his name. "Charlie. Oh, he's no trouble at all." I wondered what constituted trouble in a nursing home. Being too heavy to lift? Double incontinence? Rave parties in the corridors after midnight?

"You won't tell him, will you?" I wanted it to be a surprise.

"No, no. He'll be pleased to see you."

I drove up the M6 and then retraced the route we'd taken when I was a child. Freckleton, Warton, Lytham Green. We came for holidays, weekends, and on daytrips. The younger we were, the longer we stayed. We would drive the length of Blackpool Illuminations in the autumn, marvelling at Minnie Mouse and Road Runner hanging between the orange stars and Chinese lanterns. Charlie would take my brother and me on the pier to play the penny slot machines. Two pot dolls sat in front of milk bottles with straws. We raced the handles on each side of the glass box to see who could make the babies drink their plaster milk the fastest. Another machine had a steel claw which roved over a mound of plastic toys and sweets. When your penny dropped in the slot the claw descended and closed over the surface of the objects. Sometimes it picked up a miniature soldier or a plastic diamond ring, but usually they dropped from the claw on its way over to the chute.

I turned a corner and there was the lighthouse and the sweep of Lytham Green. No need to ask, 'Are we nearly there?' as we constantly did on those journeys. Without really thinking, I found the church, the bridge and the turning. There it stood, back from the road—The Chekita Nursing Home. The woman who'd answered the telephone opened the door. She put her fingers to her lips and took me through to the lounge. It was a huge room with a square of winged armchairs arranged in the middle. Charlie was reading a newspaper. He read for a few seconds more, then raised his head. He looked frail. Slowly, his face broke into a smile and he folded his paper onto the coffee table.

"Hello," he said, with a deep cadence. "Sit down." The owner had walked over to a sideboard at the far side of the room. She kept flicking a look over her shoulder as she made a show of scrabbling in a drawer. When she'd seen enough she left. I stepped over a very old lady and took the other chair beside him.

"I wasn't expecting . . ." he said. He took a few minutes to get used to the idea of me being there. I took a look around. The carpet was blood red with massive grey roses swirling across it. Two stunted geraniums stood on a shelf with a vase of artificial flowers. The mirror hanging over the mantelpiece had patches of brown where the silver had flaked off.

"I thought I'd come and have a look at you. I phoned up this morning."

"She never said anything."

"I asked her not to." He smiled again.

The very old lady began to stand up, take a few steps and sit down again. Stand up, take a few steps, sit down. "She's eighty-four. A bit confused." Charlie didn't bother to whisper. Her eyes were milky and her hair stood away from her head like spun sugar. She made a sequence of sounds which fell short of words. "We're the only ones in here." He paused. "I can always talk to the tropical fish!"

"How's your new hip?"

"Oh, I was suicidal with the pain. I started to think I was being pigheaded not to go private. But watch." He stood up and walked around the coffee table. Swinging his arms, he took small, steady strides. "I want to walk like a man."
He carried on walking and beckoned me from the doorway. "Come on, I'll show you my room."

I followed him along the corridor through two sets of fire doors to his room. He held open the door for me. In this, Charlie's waiting-for-his-operation-room, the window was wide open and the net curtains were flapping. Propped-up on the windowsill was one of his paintings. Apart from some photographs, it was the only object he had brought with him from home.

Charlie eased himself into the floral armchair. His eyes closed slowly and his head fell forward. I sat on the bed and listened to his soft snores.

Charlie had always painted—sea scenes and still lives in oils on carefully stretched canvases, and cartoons in black paint on his kitchen walls. At Colton House—a guesthouse he ran with his wife Millie, there was a frieze of cartoons at eye level running round the magnolia kitchen. One showed a mighty woman and a minuscule man about to be married at the altar. "Hymn number 104," pronounces the vicar, "*Fight the Good Fight*." In the next picture the same couple stand by a sink piled high with dirty dishes. The woman speaks: "Two rounds and one submission, loser washes up." Which was funny because Millie was a tiny woman and outside the church when *they* got married

Millie stood several steps up from Charlie for the photographs. Her bouquet was a cascade of sweet peas.

This painting was of one of his favourite subjects—a lone ship struggling in a turbulent sea. He'd seen plenty of tossing boats and swashbuckling waves in the Royal Navy. At Colton House he painted in the basement, where they slept in the summer season. Next to the double bed with pink candlewick bedspread was an easel; a stick with a small white cushion at the end lay across its ledge. A pot of clean brushes stood on the table beside, and the smell of linseed oil and turpentine hung in the air. After Millie died, Charlie would stay up all night to finish a battleship, a seaside cliff, or an isolated fruit bowl

Before Charlie moved to Colton House he'd been a porter at the Hotel Majestic. Guests left their shoes outside the door at night to be cleaned. If they didn't leave a tip, the next day they'd find their uppers had been gently lifted from their soles with a razor blade. Behind the bar the spirits were diluted and the difference pocketed. Charlie's next job was with the police force.

It was while he was a policeman that he boarded at Colton House. Millie was the owner's daughter. While Millie's mother lay on her deathbed she asked Charlie to marry her daughter. Charlie promised he would.

Colton House stood opposite a railway line. But after one night there I never heard the trains. Charlie would wake me with tea in a jade green cup and a digestive resting on the saucer. There were seven bedrooms and each guest had their own cupboard in the dining room. They brought their own food and there was a cruet charge for the use of pepper and salt. Seven different breakfasts and seven evening meals were cooked every day. Eventually a set menu was introduced. We phoned up one night and asked Charlie what Millie was up to. "She's dividing half a tin of fruit salad between sixteen people."

At my parents' Silver Wedding, Charlie walked in the front room wearing a thick black Beatles wig. He strutted around as if nothing was any different. The scratchy bed settee pricked my legs. There was a rubber plant I'd bought for mum almost touching the ceiling. A roar of laughter went up. Twenty people were sitting all over the floor and the air was thick with smoke. The audience bayed for more. Charlie was sat on the fireplace.

The door opened again and in walked Uncle Bill. He wasn't my real uncle. He stumbled and wobbled and fell over his feet, but we knew he wasn't quite that drunk. A bent cigarette hung out of his mouth. "There's an old seaside place called . . ." He pretended to forget. "There's an old seaside place called . . ."

The audience supplied the next word, "Blackpool."

"There's an old seaside place called Blackpool, that's noted for fresh air and fun. And Mr and Mrs Ramsbottom went there with . . ."

The audience tried to sound exasperated and filled in the rest of the line, "Young Albert their son."

"A nice little lad was young Albert." Uncle Bill stopped again and the audience was right there.

"All dressed in 'is best, quite a swell."

Bill tried to pull back this dialogue back into a monologue. "All dressed in 'is best, quite a swell. With a stick with an 'orse's 'ead 'andle." He put his finger to his mouth and screwed up his face.

The audience took the cue. "The finest that Woolworth's could sell."

They were off. Everyone recited the whole monologue while Bill tottered in front, joining in with the occasional last few words of a line. It was the same at every family gathering. We clapped ourselves and emptied our glasses while the smoke got thicker.

"Your turn now, Norman," said my Auntie Betty.

"Yes, go on," urged mum.

Dad didn't need much persuading. He sang in his soft bass voice, *"We're three little lambs and we've lost our way."* We all joined in with the refrain: *"baa, baa, baa."* Mum's smile was wide.

Next up was Uncle Jack—a real uncle. He held out a box of Pioneer matches. "How many pies on 'ere?" He turned the box over and back to show that the word 'Pioneer' written on both sides.

"Two," we all chimed.

"No, look." He held the box closer so everyone could see the steaming pie complete with air holes and fluted crust which he'd drawn on the matchbox in biro. "There's another pie on 'ere an' all." We all groaned and laughed in equal measure.

And finally Charlie got up and stood on an upturned biscuit tin which he produced from behind his back. He rocked from side to side and when he'd got his rhythm he began. "Forty-three days in a boat with only boiled ham, caviar and a McDonalds." He was completely composed. We knew that whatever he said he'd never said before and he would never say again. "The waves bashed the side of the boat till we were nearly over. We ate the caviar, boiled ham and the McDonalds. Boiled ham was best. Then a mermaid swam in from Spring Street. We pulled her in."

The wind was still whipping up the net curtains and flapping against Charlie's tossing ship when a firm knock hit the door. "Teatime!" Charlie came to and I helped him up. We walked, arm-in-arm, to the lounge. The tea was on the coffee table and the lady with the candyfloss hair had already begun.

"No buns?" she asked. Buns were Rich Tea biscuits. She was tilting her teacup as she lifted it to her mouth.

"You'll spill it," said Charlie. Wanting to take her empty cup and saucer through to the kitchen, she stood up, steadied herself against the table with one hand and picked up the cup and saucer with the other. Five times she tried this before giving up and sitting down.

"How's Doreen?" I asked.

"Don't hear much from her these days. She's busy with her jewellery business in Rye. Her son's marriage has broken up so she's giving him a home."

Charlie met Doreen while he floated round the dance floor of a cruise ship. Millie had died of cancer in her fifties. Charlie was devastated. He couldn't understand why, when so many marriages end in divorce, they couldn't have carried on being together. When he'd done with the high tide of his grieving for her he booked a berth to Australia. He wanted to see his old drinking pal who'd emigrated there; he wanted to 'swing the lamp' in the bars of Sydney.

Doreen was elegant and aloof—'a bit far back', as mum called her. When they visited my parents, reports of canoodling on the settee ricocheted round the family. I wondered how Charlie felt now about his cut-down life.

When I drove away from The Chekita, Charlie waved me off from behind the lace curtain. Always when our family left St Anne's, Charlie would stand on the street and wave until he couldn't see us anymore. His arm would be stretched way above his head and his hand swivelled round on the pivot of his wrist. He was gentle and vulnerable in equal measure to James Stewart. I adored them both.

The following year, three months before his seventy-ninth birthday, he died. In his last letter to me he said that he still had lead in his pencil. His handwriting was tall and broad shouldered.

ONYX

CORA SAT OPPOSITE THE house in her old Clio with the window wound down. She had been watching it for a couple of weeks—a bow-fronted, two-storey Georgian Grade II listed building at the beginning of the terrace. The iron railings along the low garden wall had been replaced; now number one-four-one matched the rest. The elegance of the terrace was without question, but cars and lorries left the Blackwall Tunnel roundabout and droned past the house, revving their engines so they could speed up Shooter's Hill.

It was Mondays when Cora made her pilgrimage to sit in vigil. She knew she had to establish their routine and check for any change. There was Hilary Marsden now, opening the front door, guiding the pushchair over the front doorstep and closing the door behind her. Cora looked away and quickly opened her large *A–Z*, pretending to search for a nearby street. Roy Marsden had already left for work. Hilary would now take her daughter to nursery and go on to Maze Hill station. Then the house stayed quiet till about four thirty. At four forty-five, Cora started the engine and headed for the roundabout.

'Next week should do it,' she thought. She was stiff from sitting for so long and had begun to sympathize with plain clothed policemen who had to do this for a living. A brisk stroll around Greenwich Park seemed like a good idea. When she'd lived on the top floor of one-four-one, Cora regularly walked to the park. In fact, when she first moved in she was so transfixed by the view from the Observatory that she went every evening to see the lights shine through the dusk. In daylight, depending on visibility, she could pick out Hampstead Heath. A bed of acers had recently been planted at the bottom of the Astronomer's Garden. Cora stood for a while, captivated by their autumn burnish of burgundy and rust.

She now lived in Hither Green. Only one item from her days of renting the furnished top floor flat remained in her possession—a two-bar electric fire. She liked the arch of silver behind the two elements; she had never seen one with such a high elegant curve. The day the van came to remove her belongings to Hither Green was the day *before* she was due to leave. For the last night she slept without sheets on the single bed. She lay on her back and remembered all the times she had laid awake thinking, 'When will this end? How will this end? Will there be another setting for the next stage of my life?' She turned to face the wall and closed her eyes.

The next morning she ate the remnants of her Indian takeaway for breakfast. Roy Marsden took the day off work, thinking this would be the day she moved out. He didn't want her getting away with the circular mahogany table or the set of household brushes. Cora was glad she had fooled him.

"You could shit in the corner when you leave," said Cora's friend, Beth. "Or introduce cockroaches to the fabric of the building." It was Beth that Cora usually phoned when the going got tough.

"Have you got a few minutes?" she asked Beth.

"As long as you like. Let me just turn the gas off and get my cup of tea." Beth clicked and clattered in the background. "What's happened?"

"Do you remember he said I couldn't have plants on my landing window?"

"Yes."

"He's put paint stripper in them."

"No!"

"They've all wilted and died. Three shades of pink geraniums. Cuttings from my gran."

"I *am* sorry."

"And that's not all." Cora's voice escalated. "He's padlocked my bike to the back stairs."

"Never! What will you do?"

"I don't know!"

When Cora discovered that friends who called her on the payphone in the hall were being told she'd moved out six weeks ago, she had her own phone installed in her back room. A couple of days later, she picked up the handset and couldn't get a dialling tone. 'Typical,' she thought. 'I get my first phone and it won't work.' She trudged to the payphone on the corner to report the fault. Walking back up the front garden path, she noticed the phone lines on the vast side wall of the house. There was Marsden's — grimy, old and black; and there was hers — shiny, new and navy blue. At shoulder height there was a three-inch gap in her wire. She could see the copper inside the flex where it had been snipped.

Friends who came to stay were accosted on the stairs. "You can't stay here overnight you know. It's not allowed." He'd announce his orders and remove himself before anyone had a chance to reply. Cora knew that if she'd been a man they'd have come to blows months ago. She wished she could pack a punch which would send him flying down the three flights of stairs.

The funny thing was that they had lived happily as neighbours for two years—sharing a bathroom, politely declining invitations to each others' parties, both putting fifty pence coins in the gas boiler to heat the bathwater. Until, that is, the house came on the market and the Marsdens bought it for a song, with Cora as a sitting tenant. Then the Marsdens waited for Cora to feed money into the boiler and used up what was left. Cora would sit in the bath feeling furious. In the opposite wall were three small holes which had been filled up with Polyfilla. A previous tenant has drilled them to get a look at his neighbour in the bath.

After a particularly strenuous day's teaching, Cora went into the bathroom. The bath was filled to the top, on her money. Curls of steam lifted from the surface in smug smiles. Cora pulled the plug out, ran upstairs and locked herself in. It was the only time she retaliated.

The house rose in value to a quarter of a million. Cora

calculated that she was therefore worth sixty-two and a half thousand pounds, given that a sitting tenant lowered the price of a property by a quarter. On a cool September day, Roy Marsden knocked on her door. His face was pale and his hair was greasy. He didn't bother to smile or greet her, but stood awkwardly in the doorway shooting glances around the room. She had recently bought a low round basketwork table which sat beneath the window. Cora steeled herself.

"I have a friend," he began, "who would like to move into this flat. *We* would like him to move in. He is prepared to pay more than you pay in rent. If you move out, we will pay you half the difference between what he pays and what you pay."

"No. No way," said Cora. Her voice was weak. Indignation hadn't yet risen in her and she felt invaded by his visit.

"Have it your own way. And we don't want you bringing your own furniture in here," he said pointing to the new table. He turned and went downstairs, two stairs at a time.

Cora flopped onto her chair. She couldn't believe it! For how long did he propose paying her the difference? What was his friend prepared to pay? What recourse would she have if he didn't pay her? He must think she was very naïve. She had registered her rent with the council long before the Marsdens had arrived. Surely this should give her some protection? For the 'nth time Cora considered her options. Not enough points for a council place, no joy with housing associations, not enough money to buy or rent on the open market. She banged her fists on the arms of the chair and gazed out at the turning trees and the distant dome of St Paul's.

She was dammed if she was going to spend any more of her time earning money to pay rent. She may not have the latest sound equipment, but what she did have was time. Time to rub soft pastels across textured paper, time to photograph the floor of Oxleas Woods, time to bake a Bakewell tart. She was paid well enough to support herself on the three days a week that she taught literacy skills at the local college. The rest could wait.

After yet another incident, Beth met Cora in the gazebo café in the park. Cora looked pale, drained of her usual easy colour. "What's happened now?" asked Beth.

"He left a radio playing at full blast outside my door."

"What did you do?"

"I called the police. I bolted to the front door when I heard the bell."

"I bet he didn't like that!"

"He followed us up the stairs! He reckoned he'd been hoovering and he forgot! He wriggled like a schoolboy."

"At least now he knows you're not going to take everything lying down."

"It did feel good to have those two burly men in helmets stood right next to me."

Beth took a sip of her coffee. Sparrows were pecking at crumbs on the outside tables. "Why don't you just move out?"

"Because it's my home! I've a right to be there! He doesn't seem to understand that. I asked him for a rent book and he refused to give me one. He said it would strengthen my position. But my position couldn't be any stronger if I *did* have a rent book."

Beth could see that Cora was adamant, and she was probably right, but she was concerned about the effects this protracted battle was having on Cora.

"Want to go and see a film?" Beth asked.

"As long as it's not Tarkovsky."

A few days later a note appeared underneath Cora's door. Marsden had written it in green biro; his handwriting was thin and leaned to the left. *We are offering you the generous sum of five hundred pounds to move out.* Cora screwed it up, threw it in the bin and kicked the sideboard. The following week a solicitor's letter arrived. 'Let battle commence,' thought Cora.

She found her own solicitor in Yellow Pages. There were parlour palms and up-to-date magazines in the foyer. Her solicitor had tightly curled hair and photographs of her daughter on her desk. In one of them her daughter had her finger up her nose. "If you'd like to fill in this green form we'll be able to apply for legal aid for you. If you get legal aid and the case goes to court, you'll be entitled to a barrister."

A letter arrived for Cora from her solicitor one morning to explain that Marsden's solicitor had found a loophole in the law. *Mr Marsden would be within his rights to purchase a flat and offer it to you as suitable alternative accommodation. In fact this is what he is in the process of doing.* The letter gave the address of the property. It was a basement flat further down the road. Cora went to have a look.

The flat was part of a Victorian terrace, bang next to a petrol station. The front door was obscured from view because it was sunk below ground level. The sign outside said 'Under Offer'. Cora climbed down the steps. It appeared to be empty. There was a sticker— BEWARE OF THE DOG —on the door, with a picture of an Alsatian baring its teeth. Cora peered through the glass front door. The room was very small and very dark. When she was visited by her solicitor and her barrister, she got to see inside.

"Well, it's less floor space than you have now," said the barrister. His hair was even more tightly curled than Cora's solicitor's.

"And there is very little natural light. Which we can argue that, since you are an artist, you need," said her solicitor.

"How do you feel about a court appearance, Cora?" asked the barrister.

Before Cora could answer her solicitor said, "She will give very good evidence."

To Cora's huge relief, a court case was avoided. Marsden bought the flat but realized he would loose money if he went to court and lost. *Mr Marsden intends,* said the next letter, *having taken advice, to sell his current purchase and to buy another flat which will comply with the terms of suitable alternative accommodation; whereupon you will be required to move. He is willing, as an alternative, to offer you the sum of £20,000 to settle the matter. Please advise me of your instructions.* It was now five years since the Marsdens had bought the property. Marsden's wife was pregnant with her first child.

Cora found a flat, a mortgage and, for the first time in her life, she had proper neighbours. Neighbours who came to introduce themselves, neighbours who cut the hedge which ran between the two front gardens, neighbours who invited her to dinner. She stood underneath her shower and watched a grey squirrel taking a walk along the top of the fence. She sat in the front room of her ground floor flat and listened to an ice cream van playing *Greensleeves*, or a rag and bone man shouting 'Any old iron!' It felt like the suburbs compared to Shooter's Hill Road.

She couldn't have been more content. She grew ladybird poppies and grape hyacinth, she painted the walls pink, she stripped floors and doorframes and hunted down a discarded primary school sink for her bathroom. But Marsden gnawed at her. He had got off too easily. The money didn't compensate for the invasion, the constant anxiety, the disavowal of her home.

The following Monday, Cora waited until Hilary Marsden had trollied out her daughter, then she drove off the main road and parked. She still had a key to the front door. She had returned one key to Marsden but had kept her spare. The question was—would he have changed the locks? She put on her thin cotton gloves.

The gold coloured key fitted straight into the gold coloured lock. She closed the door gently, released the snick to lock herself in, and went upstairs. She wanted to see her old rooms. The louvered attic window which she had covered with clingfilm every winter had been replaced by a double glazed unit. The kitchen area had been ripped out along with the brown lino. Still standing in the back room was the substantial double wardrobe which she'd piled with jumpers, tennis rackets and old shoes. The garden had been landscaped—gone was the rectangle of lawn with beds of nothing down either side. There was now a patio with white cast iron furniture and strategically-placed shrubs.

On the next landing down, the bathroom had been knocked through to make a bigger bedroom. Cora remembered coming home one evening to find two bodies outside the bathroom and three on the stairs. The Marsdens were having a party. The guests who were too drunk to carry on had slithered down the walls and lay slumped in uncomfortable positions. If they wanted her to feel an intruder in her own home they succeeded. Cora went into the bedroom. She carefully turned down the silk quilt on the double bed and left a chocolate praline snail on each pillow.

The front room on the ground floor had been decorated while she still lived there. If the door was slightly open as she made her way to the front door, she could see a basket of logs on one side of the fireplace and an arrangement of onyx eggs on the other. It was still exactly the same.

Downstairs in the basement kitchen, Cora opened all the drawers and cupboards. She pulled out a yellow cotton table-cloth and threw it up in the air to land on the dining table. Then she laid six place settings with cutlery, glasses and napkins. She took the candelabra from the window sill and lit the two red candles with the gas lighter from the cooker. From the rack standing beside the back door she chose two bottles of Frascati and placed them in the door of the fridge. She turned on the radio, set it to Classic FM, and went back upstairs.

Standing for a moment beside the floor-to-ceiling windows, she could touch the original panelled shutters, folded to the sides. Cora took three long strides then jumped towards the fire-place. A box of matches was propped against an ashtray on the mantelpiece. She lit the screwed-up newspaper which jutted from the grate, and when the criss-cross of kindling began to roar, she added four logs from the basket.

The onyx eggs were sitting in a circle on a glass-topped table. Cora picked the clearest egg with the least amount of brown marbling through the green and put it in her pocket. She placed the fireguard carefully on the hearth, and left.

The egg found a home in her wide Spanish fruit dish, along-side some kiwi fruit and a conference pear. When the dish was empty, the egg stood alone, like a stone in a desert of sand.

UNSAID

BEFORE SHE LEFT HER flat for the evening, Clara cut out two photographs from a brochure for the Cheltenham Literature Festival—one of herself, and one of Nick. They were due to read on consecutive nights in October. She placed the photographs side-by-side in a picture frame she'd been given for Christmas. It was encrusted with opalescent stones round the circumference. When she was satisfied with their arrangement, she placed the frame on her bedside table and lit it with her old brass angle-poise, glancing at the two smiling black and white faces as she closed the bedroom door.

That night Nick was launching his latest volume of poems. It had been seven years since his last collection and his new book held the promise of greatness. Tickets were sold out. Clara knew that she would almost definitely meet Philippa that night—Nick's new partner. Well, not so new in fact—partner of six years. Four years ago he'd been seeing Philippa *and* Clara. Sure, he'd given Clara clues that she wasn't the only player on his field, but Clara's perception was filtered through faulty equipment—she received the satellite information, but only processed it three months later. So when Nick phoned one day to say he could only see her in the afternoons, she was flattened. "She was in extremis," said Nick. "I had to let her stay. Don't get upset . . . OK, you can phone me whenever you like."

In the months which followed, Clara came to realize that what this meant was that Philippa had left her husband and moved in with Nick. Clara was relegated to lunch at the South Bank, or tea at Madam Berteaux. And though on those occasions Nick was always attentive—kissing her before he got up to order more drinks, kissing her hand through the window before she drove off in her car—he never again came to her flat in Camberwell carrying presents of Schubert and scarves.

After three of these meetings, neither of them suggested another. Their relationship had gone backwards. They had progressed to chaste dates during the day. They were like a fire in a hearth—the newspaper had caught but it failed to ignite the kindling. Clara concluded that, for better or worse, Philippa must be what Nick needed; he hadn't loved Clara enough. She had been too full of doubts to fight for him—doubts about him, doubts about being able to compete with his literary standing. He had published four collections to her one, he had been shortlisted for the T.S. Eliot Prize *and* he was a Fellow of the Royal Society of Literature. Some or all of these had got in the way.

After that, Clara had a transatlantic flurry with a gallery curator in New York, but it floundered when he asked her to move across the water. When it came to it there was nowhere else she wanted to live but London. She adored her flat. She'd spent hours looking for the right porcelain door handles; she'd travelled miles to find brass bottle taps for her roll top bath. Being alone didn't bother her. She had friends, she had her work, and she liked to be able to please herself. She managed to forget what it was like to be close to someone.

Clara parked on a single yellow line on Long Acre. She tweaked her fringe in the rear view mirror and applied another layer of lipstick, then she tipped her chin upwards to check the smoothness of her throat. It was a relief to her that the fairness of her hair hid the silver grey which was starting to appear, or so she thought. The day before, Clara had phoned Nick to ask if he would write a reference for her for a fellowship. She had known about the launch for weeks and she wondered if he would mention it.

"I have a reading tomorrow. At Betterton Street."

"Oh?" said Clara.

"I haven't invited many people. We're going to have supper afterwards. Do you think you might come?"

"I'll see how I'm fixed."

Clara walked past Covent Garden tube and up Endell Street. It was July and diners and drinkers had taken to the streets. The air was thick with humidity, begging for a storm. She went up to the Poetry Café window and peered through a clear strip between the etched glass. Nick was standing by a table—tall, white-haired, solicitous of the woman he was talking to. Clara turned on her heels and walked back the way she'd come. She needed more time. She knew that all her wonderings over the last four years about Philippa and Nick would be realized that night. She did a circuit round the block till she felt calmer. Then she pushed open the glass door and walked between the wooden tables and chairs to where Nick was sitting. He stood up as soon as he saw her and kissed her cheek. "You came!" Extricating himself from the table, he walked with her to the bar. "What would you like?"

"White wine, please," smiled Clara. She wasn't quite sure yet which one at Nick's table was Philippa, but so far she was pleased with her reception.

They sat down and Nick made a general introduction. "This is Clara May." Clara spread a magnanimous smile round the table. She guessed Philippa was the neat, dark-haired woman to Nick's left—mid-forties, fine skin, unsmiling. Clara looked down at her black velvet blouse and realised that she had left the top two buttons unfastened. She turned to the man to her right.

"Are you Hal Morris?"

"Yes, how do you know?"

"I saw a photograph in *Poetry News* last year—you won the National." Hal nodded with pleasure. He looked much more interesting than his photograph—softer and altogether less serious. Clara liked the fact that he seemed unaware of his celebrity.

At seven thirty everyone climbed the stairs for Nick's reading. Afterwards, behind the book-signing queue, Philippa met Clara's gaze for the first time, then she quickly looked away.

They walked in a group to a trattoria in Bloomsbury. It was a cheerful gingham-tabled place playing snatches of Carmen and Rigoletto. Clara made sure that she sat between Hal and

Richard. Richard was an old university friend of Nick's—a motorbike-riding lawyer.

"What would you like?" Philippa asked Nick. "There's chicken in a wine sauce, grilled fish, carbonara. You like carbonara."

"Is there any steak?" asked Nick.

"Yes," replied Philippa, slightly surprised.

"I'll have steak," said Nick, with satisfaction.

"Or there's cannelloni?" Philippa went on.

"Steak will do me fine. Rare."

"But you usually like it well done." Philippa looked disconcerted. Nick wasn't sticking to form—or the form that she knew.

"I'll have steak too," said Hal. "What about you, Clara?"

"I'm going to have lasagne," said Philippa.

"I'll have the risotto," said Clara. "Because it takes so long to cook if you do it yourself." Clara thought about what she'd just said. "Well, not that long, but you have to stand over it."

"And I'll have the ossobuco," said Richard, " because I like the sound of the word. Can't stand veal though." Only Philippa didn't laugh.

The waitress placed a basket of bread and a saucer of olive oil between Clara and Hal. They began to dip and chew. "I'm looking at a flat in Herne Hill at nine o'clock in the morning," said Nick.

"You're moving to South London?" asked Clara.

"No. I live in Norfolk. I'm after a property to rent out. I've just sold a house in Diss and I'm hoping to clean up with the capital," said Hal.

"*In* the capital," said Clara.

"That's about it. I need to make some money. I've a new son. And my daughter's still at school." Clara's eyes rested on Hal for rather longer than was necessary. She was always puzzled by other people's responsibilities.

"Do you think we should offer the bread around?" suggested Clara, aware that they were eating most of it.

"No, let them fend for themselves," said Hal. "You're not from the south are you?"

"No, Lancashire. My father says I need to keep going home to learn how to talk proper," said Clara flattening her accent. "Did you go to public school?"

"Is it that obvious?" Hal didn't sound too surprised.

And so Hal and Clara began to make a world for themselves—a place where they had their own food and conversation, where they explored the reaches of each other's lives. "I had a friend I used to go clubbing with. We played 'pubic schoolboy spotting'."

"What did you do when you spotted one?" Hal asked.

"We'd go up and check. We were never wrong. Something about the ready smile, the straight back, healthy complexion. And always an easy way with words. Consonants slipping under the tongue," said Clara in a measured, gentle tone.

"Hmm," said Hal, not sure if this was a compliment or not.

"What happened to your friend?" asked Hal.

"How do you mean?" said Clara, tilting her head.

"You said you *had* a friend."

"Oh! She turned gay and I didn't fit into her life anymore," Clara said with resignation. The basket of bread was now empty.

"There's nothing behind her eyes," said Nick.

"Whose?" asked Clara, realising that she and Hal hadn't been taking part in the general conversation.

"Nigella Lawson's. How can you call a book *How To Eat*? Doesn't she think we know how to eat?" Philippa said something which Clara couldn't quite hear.

"Philippa likes Nigella's recipes," announced Nick on her behalf.

"I'm starving," said Richard, glancing at the empty breadbasket. Just then the waitress brought their dishes. Philippa seemed to be questioning Nick earnestly, but all Clara could hear was Nick saying, "Let's sort it out when we get home." Clara watched Nick planting kisses on Philippa's lips and cheeks and remembered when he'd been affectionate to her—on trains, in bars, in car parks. Then she thought about the fact that Hal was staying with Nick that night and that Nick lived in Ealing.

"How are you going to get to that flat for nine o'clock in the morning?" she asked. They'd already drunk three bottles of wine. "Where I live is just down the road from Herne Hill."

"Do you have a spare room?" asked Hal.

"Not as such," said Clara, slowly.

"This conversation *was* quite promising," said Hal.

"I have a back room, and a kind of spare bed," offered Clara.

"Are you sure you wouldn't mind?" Hal wanted to make sure he was welcome.

"Of course not."

"We have an announcement to make," said Hal to the table.

"You two are getting married?" teased Richard.

Hal ignored the joke. "I'm going to be staying at Clara's place tonight. It's close to Herne Hill. Where the flat is I'm supposed to see at nine."

"You must do what you want," said Nick.

Nick and Hal became disinterested in eating and didn't finish their meals. Nick didn't light up a cigarette, as Clara would have expected. "I gave up eight months ago," he said.

"Did you use those patches?" asked Clara.

"Why poison myself with what I'm trying to rid my body of?"

At ten thirty Philippa got up to leave saying she had an early start for work in the morning. "See you back at home," she said to Nick kissing him three times. She made sure he knew exactly the number of the bus to get back to Ealing and the precise location of the bus stop.

'There it is,' thought Clara. 'I could never have done that, spent my life managing Nick.'

"So, you're not coming back to ours?" Philippa asked Hal. "I won't see you?" She seemed unable to grasp the situation and kissed him on the cheek. Philippa had managed not to look at Clara, nor to speak to her throughout the whole meal. Only when she stood in the doorway did Philippa say one word to Clara. 'Goodbye.'

Almost as soon as the door closed the conversation turned to sex. Nick and Richard had a mutual friend they knew from university who had been celibate for several years.

"I can't imagine not wanting to fuck someone," said Nick. Clara laughed out loud. It was easier to forgive him when he was being transparent. After cappuccinos and crispy mints they paid the bill and left. Nick kissed Clara on the cheek and went to find his bus.

"Goodbye, lovebirds," said Richard, pulling on his motorbike gear and submerging his head in his helmet. Hal and Clara walked back to her car.

"Are you sure this is OK?" asked Hal.

"Sure," said Clara. "I wouldn't have offered if it wasn't."

Clara swept along the roads and darted in and out of the little traffic that there was. On Waterloo Bridge they could see veins of lightning routed between the London Eye and Tate Modern. Within half an hour Clara was parking deftly in the only space left on her street. "Very good bit of driving," said Hal. "I'm a nervous driver, myself."

Just as they stepped out of the car, huge drops of warm rain began to fall. More rain fell in the time it took to get to the front door than had fallen in the previous two weeks. Clara switched on the lights, locked the front door after them, and grabbed a towel from the bathroom. The shoulders of Hal's olive green polo shirt had darkened with the rain. She left him rubbing his hair in the kitchen while she hurried into the bedroom. Now that Clara had met Philippa she felt that she and Nick had a full stop and a line drawn beneath them. She took the picture frame from by the bed and hid it in under the newspapers in the log basket. When the kettle had boiled, Hal helped her carry a tray of coffee and a bottle of Jameson's into the back room.

"This is a lovely flat," he said as he walked through and saw a door which led into a small conservatory. Clara picked up a new bottle-green watering can which stood on her worktable.

"This is my pride and joy," she said.

"Yes, I was looking at that." The spout was an elegant arc, which finished in a brass rose with tiny holes.

"It can give a very fine sprinkle." There was a pause then they both laughed.

Clara had never met anyone who knew Nick well. She told him their history. "So you two were an item?" When she told him about Nick's afternoon-only rule, he said, "That's not a solution." But he wasn't surprised at how things had gone. "It's the way Nick is. He behaves badly, then everyone forgives him."

He had no criticism of Philippa. "She's part of the Nick package now. You see Nick, you see Philippa. She's kept him on the straight. I bumped into him at the World Service before she moved in. He was drunk as a lord at nine thirty in the morning."

"I couldn't have done that," said Clara. "I need a father, not to have to mother someone."

"Her husband was rich but dull. Nick is poor but never dull."

"How do they manage?"

"Philippa's training to be a physiotherapist. She didn't need to work before."

"I suppose one has to admire her for that," said Clara, grudgingly. Then she remembered something that Nick had told her in one of their last meetings.

"Not everyone forgives Nick. Did you know his last partner—Jenny?"

"I knew of her," said Hal.

"She got cancer—after Nick and her split up. They'd lived together for six years. She refused to see Nick—even when she was on her deathbed. He was very cut up about it. He would lie beside Philippa and cry and call out Jenny's name."

"He told you all this?" asked Hal, surprised.

"Yes."

"It must have ended badly."

After a couple of glasses of whisky and an Arvo Pärt CD, Clara began to prepare Hal's bed. A comfy, precarious arrangement of cushions from the blue water silk sofa with a baby futon balanced on the top. Hal stood by as he watched Clara building his bed. "My grandma's embroidered sheet," said Clara as she threw it up to catch the air so that it would fall flat on the futon. She piled a duvet and blankets over the pillows, hoping that the combination would be comfortable.

When Clara said goodnight she stood in the hall and kept Hal at a distance. "Help yourself to towels or whatever you need." Hal simply looked back at her. When she thought back to these moments she realised that Hal hadn't spoken for some time. He stood, motionless, looking at her with his clear grey eyes. His fine boyish hair was already dry.

Clara sat on her bed in her blue and white striped cotton pyjamas. She felt she had lived for a year that evening. She tried to read but kept going over and over the same paragraph. She knew it would take her at least an hour to fall asleep. But at least, she thought, Hal must have settled; the bathroom sounds and the walking to and fro had stopped.

Clara put down her book, lay back with her knees bent and closed her eyes. A loud determined rap came on her door. Her body jumped. Clara climbed off the bed and opened the door. Hal was standing there, gesturing with his palm open towards her. "There's something I have to tell you," he said.

"What?"

"You have a great bathroom."

"Thank you," Clara said automatically.

"And I want you to know—we're both adults, and I think it would be a shame if I were to sleep in there and you were to sleep in here."

"You don't have to say that. It's not what's expected of you."

Hal walked a little way towards her. "No, I know. I don't mean that. I wanted to say, I wouldn't want it to go unsaid . . . I think you're great."

"But you're married, with children. You have a new baby."

"I'm not married."

"You live with someone?"

"Yes."

"What is her name?"

"Megan."

"And what are your children's names?"

"Freya and Max."

"Hal, I've only just met you. I may never see you again."

"I see what you're saying."

"Go to bed," pleaded Clara putting her arms around him. Hal's arms closed around her. They stood next to Clara's wardrobe, stroking each other's back and shoulders.

"I guess this will have to do," said Hal.

Clara lay awake for most of that night. She was right wasn't she, that spending the night with Hal would have left her feeling as vulnerable as a victim of third degree burns? The next day he would travel back to his family. She would have to imagine him being welcomed home . . . answering questions. How would he construe his visit? Besides, she'd had enough one night stands to know that wasn't what she wanted. And though she'd only just met Hal, she knew it wasn't what she wanted with him. But the entire surface of her body was flayed with longing. She almost wished that he *had* left things unsaid—she could have carried on in her own cocoon. But Hal had bridged the distance which could have kept them from each other.

She longed to go next door and drag him from his bed. She turned over onto her stomach, drew her fists under her shoulders and pressed her body hard into the mattress. Only when the light crept around the sides of the Roman blinds did she fall into fitful sleep.

QUEEN OF SHEBA

MR CHOZEN SPENDS HIS winters in the summer of his seed cat-
alogues. In spring, though he is grateful for the lime green of
his euphorbias, he's already anticipating the russet of his flame
bush in the fall. His garden is the backdrop to his busy life. If he
has to travel from Forest Hill to Enfield to rep books for his company, he can carry with him the yellow edges of his red Queen of
Sheba tulips. In one particularly difficult meeting with a manager who had no interest whatsoever in military history, he got
a sudden flash of his acid yellow witch hazel—in stark silhou-
ette against next-door's dark leylandii.

As the roofs and spires of South East London sped past the
train window on his way home, the leylandii grew wider in his
mind until it reached the South Circular to the north and the
Quaggy River to the south. The image stayed in his mind as his
frustration grew with the young bookshop manager. Mr Chozen
couldn't understand how, in less than a generation, shelf life
for the veterans and POWs of the Second World War had given
way to celebrity chefs and water features. The leylandii was now
growing taller in his mind than the adjacent poplars. His neighbours had fled to a hillside in Wales. They let out their property
to music students and no longer cared about the nuisance
they'd left behind.

Just the year before, Mr Chozen had made a pilgrimage to
Kanchanaburi. He visited the bridge over the River Kwai, looking down as he walked its length past the rows of sleepers to the

rushing water beneath. He found his uncle's grave in the War Cemetery—a small grey tablet surrounded by low growing pink roses—PRIVATE W.J. DAY. AGE 22. JUST SLEEPING. He visited the Jeath Museum with its reconstructed POW camp and saw the simple bed where his uncle might have laid his head. The drawings pinned to the walls were made on tissue-thin scraps of paper—emaciated men, corpses strewn along the ground.

The train stopped at Forest Hill. Mr Chozen rose to his feet and hugged his briefcase under his arm. It wasn't as if he hadn't tried to do something about the tree. He'd made phone calls to the managing agent, he'd written letters ... but nothing changed. The tree continued to block the light, disallowing any rays to pass through as the sun dipped behind.

The sky was becoming dark. Mr Chozen hurried home to avoid the forecast storm. His wife wasn't back yet. He often had this hour to himself. The students next door weren't back from college, so there wasn't the sound of flute and French horn high in the air; car alarms usually heralded the evening. The kettle reached a crescendo and clicked itself off. As he poured the water onto a teabag, he noticed a set of keys, as if for the first time, hanging from a hook. They were the keys for next door, with an especially long silver key for the side gate.

A welcome spell of warm weather followed. Mr Chozen kept an eye on the forecast to see how long it was expected to last. He imagined the sun drying out the tree as he took his daily journeys around the capital. On the sixth day of warmth, in his quiet solitary hour, he took his car to the local petrol station and filled up the red canister which usually lay empty in his boot. There was a basket full of sticks next to the fireplace left over from winter. He took these with the petrol and a box of extra long matches and let himself into next door's garden.

Mainly shrubs and a clumsy rockery, the garden had been designed for ease of maintenance. It was monochrome compared to Mr Chozen's choices, until he lit the carefully laid petrol-soaked sticks at the base of the tree. The flames licked up the trunk of the leylandii and ripped through the lower branches, reminding him of the yellow edges on the red petals of his Queen of Sheba tulips.

BETWEEN HERE AND KNITWEAR

THE NEW YEAR HAD started. Myra wanted to smash the glass and china display at Allder's sale; the Croydon branch was dense with discounts and offers. Pyramids of bulging red wine glasses and ladders of flutes were asking for it. There was a particularly cocky arrangement of Royal Doulton seconds—fine white china with gold rims, which definitely had it coming.

It wasn't as if Christmas had been an out and out disaster. The day had begun with Jacques Loussier playing Bach, and a little snow—a fine flurry settling on the night's frost. Myra sorted through the albums in her parents' radiogram—James Last and his Orchestra, Herb Alpert and his Tijuana Brass, Kiri te Kanawa. She stacked-up likely contenders to play through the day.

She had driven up from London the day before. By the time she hit Ramsbottom, the Victorian Fayre was putting its stalls away. The Christmas lights over the shops were delicate and fleeting, unlike the clumsy lumpen lights she had left behind in Lewisham.

The bungalow looked the same as ever—solid and snug like a familiar illustration in a children's book. The garden was overgrown—the trees and shrubs were indistinguishable from one another, and the plastic urns were blown over onto their sides.

Myra picked up two bottles of milk from the doorstep and took them in with her. Her mother had taken to keeping odd items in the fridge—a packet of sugar, a box of dried lasagne, a bag of boiled sweets. Myra pulled them out. "It's damp in the cupboards," protested her mother.

It took a while for Myra to slot into the mode of her mother's home. The kitchen floor and the bathroom floor were filthy. "Hasn't your cleaner been?" asked Myra.

"Sonia? She wouldn't come."

"Why not?"

"She wouldn't come while the decorators were here. She didn't want to clean everything and then . . ."

". . . it all get dirty again." Myra often finished off her mother's sentences.

The newly papered walls undulated with seven designs of anaglypta; but the curtains were rolled-up on the beds, and her mother's ornaments, pictures and mirrors were boxed-up in the sunroom. Her mother called it 'the conservatory.' To Myra, a conservatory was a splendour of Victorian glass built into a beautiful shape. But her mother was proud of her perspex extension, even if now it did only house dried flowers and a couple of intrepid geraniums.

Her mother had tried to replace the brass swans and the Dick Turpin toby jug on the shelves by the fireplace, but her arthritis soon sent her into her high-backed chair with a hot water bottle.

When Jacques Loussier finished, Myra put on Maura Lympany playing Chopin waltzes and got out the mop and bucket. "Do it on Boxing Day," pleaded her mother.

"I'm not having Christmas Day with dirty floors," said Myra. She couldn't say, 'I'm not having Christmas dinner with dirty floors', because they were due to go out for their festive meal. They had an invitation. From Gorsey Clough.

Myra screwed the grey mop round in the sieve of the orange plastic bucket and dragged it across the kitchen floor. The Chopin was jumping over the scratches on the LP. As the piano swelled towards crescendos, Myra swathed the floors with grey water. She stroked and soaked and smoothed the floors until all that was left were the burn marks on the lino where her mother had dropped cigarettes. She had started to smoke when she was fifteen. At seventy-four she wasn't about to give up.

"There was a tune I liked on Desert Island Discs. Was it yesterday? Slaves. She was a writer."

"Not an astrologer?" Myra had heard the same programme.

"Yes, that was it."

"Verdi."

"Might have been."

"You can see the dust when the sun shines," said her mother. She spoke slowly and deliberately, each word an effort. There were frequent pauses and hesitations. Pauses which Myra's answer machine back in London did not have patience for. She would often get home to a message of her mother's heavy breathing.

Myra found a feather duster in the umbrella stand and set about the sideboard, flicking a pathway through the dust on the mahogany surface. Six frosted highball glasses stood next to a Capo di Monte figure who was frying an egg on his knee.

Gorsey Clough was a residential care home in Tottington. Myra's father had lived there for eight months. If Myra and her mother arrived by eleven forty-five, they could eat Christmas dinner with him. Myra put on her make-up—the same make-up she'd been wearing for fifteen years. She occasionally replaced a dried-up mascara, or tried out a new slimline lipstick, but mostly she stuck with what she knew. Her mother put on a pair of lace-up shoes instead of the slippers which she usually wore inside and out for comfort.

Myra made a quick phone call. She wanted to hear David's voice. They'd been together for five years. They hadn't wanted to spend Christmas apart, but their parents were at opposite ends of the country. He was attending to his parents in Edenbridge. "Happy Christmas, Myra."

"Happy Christmas, David."

"Is it?"

"Too early to say. I'll tell you later."

David's parents were slightly younger, more mobile and more a part of the world than Myra's. They did line dancing, drove a new car and went on holiday to Majorca. Myra envied them their quality of life on her parents' behalf.

By the time Myra escorted her mother to the car, the water which she had earlier dribbled over her windscreen had frozen into a rivulet on the path. "What's that?" asked her mother, pointing. "Is your car leaking?"

Gorsey Clough was an old coaching house—blackened stone walls and dependable windows. It could've been a scene from a Bronte novel—women moving gracefully in long frocks, horses trotting on the wet cobbles. Instead it was home for the forgotten and the forlorn. The cars that were in the carpark mostly belonged to the staff.

Her father was sitting in the lounge—the second lounge, for the badly behaved. Not that it was their fault. But the residential home residents wouldn't put up with a continuous loop of shouting, or impromptu urination from the 'mentally infirm' residents.

"Harry, you've got visitors," said Peter. Peter was a familiar member of staff to Myra and her mother. He always smiled and was quick to offer a tray of tea. He kissed them both though Myra didn't feel comfortable with this physical-affection-because-it-was-Christmas. Her father stirred and tried to turn round. His eyes were milky and wet.

"Hello," said her mother brightly, trying to jog him into recognition. Her father grabbed her mother's hand.

"Could we open presents in his room?" Myra asked Peter.

"Of course." He led the way and unlocked the door of her father's room. Her father and mother ambled along the corridor, arm-in-arm.

The bedclothes were bunched up near the top of the bed. The pillows lay side by side on the floor. Myra raised her hand to her nose and mouth to stifle the smell of urine. "Shall I open the window?" asked Peter.

"Yes, please," said Myra. Neither of them referred to the smell.

"Sorry, we haven't done this room yet. I'll get someone to come. Would you like more chairs?" He wedged the door of the room open and went in search of furniture.

Myra's mother manoeuvred herself into the armchair and heaved a sigh of relief. Peter returned with two extra upright chairs. He guided her father so that the back of his legs were touching the seat of the armchair. "Sit down now, Harry. Sit down. Bend your legs."

Now that her father was standing, he was reluctant to abandon himself to sitting. It took a huge leap of faith for him to believe that the chair would be there if he surrendered to it. "Sit down, Harry. That's it." Her father's legs gave way and the chair caught him.

Myra marvelled at Peter. *She* had never known what to say to her father; how to get him to sit at the table instead of endlessly hovering. She had thought him obtuse and difficult. She hadn't seen that he needed help, words of instruction, words of encouragement. "When I got him up this morning I told him it was Christmas Day. He said, 'I must buy a box of chocolates for my wife.' He's lovely. Aren't you, Harry? He's no trouble." Peter tousled her father's hair as though he was six years old. Then he quickly made the bed and left.

Her father's hair had been cut into an uncharacteristic style. Usually he wore it combed back, neat, off his forehead. Here they combed it forward to look like Frank Sinatra in his later years.

"You've got some cards," said her mother. Myra rearranged them on the melamine chest of drawers. "Who are they from?" There was a hint of jealousy in her mother's voice. This was part of her husband's life she didn't know about.

"This one's from the home," said Myra, trying to clear up the mystery. "This one's from David and me. The rest are from the family." Myra placed another card from her basket on the chest. It was from their neighbour. The neighbour had bothered to write out two cards—one for her mother and one for her father; but her mother had automatically put them both on the mantelpiece. Myra was determined that her father should have what little was due to him.

"I don't want to lose you," her father said to her mother. "I don't want you to marry someone else." Her mother stroked his hand.

"It's all right," she said.

"Here's a present for you, dad." Myra passed him a golden parcel from her basket. Her father looked down at it but didn't know what to do. Myra helped him to pull at the Sellotape. He was concerned about damaging the wrapping paper. It was a green cardigan fleece with a nametape stitched inside the neckline.

A woman appeared at the door—she was the laundry manager. "Do you mind if I do his clothes?" She came in and filed some garments in the wardrobe. Myra pointed out the new cardigan, and the nametape. "I really appreciate that," said the laundry lady. Some of her father's clothes found their way back to him, some didn't. Garments tended to circulate, and Myra had seen her father in navy blue jogging bottoms and a lemon roll-neck sweater; items he suited well enough but which he would never have chosen to wear.

"It's a bit cold in here," said the laundry lady walking over to the window. She shut it and left. Myra got up and opened it again.

Her father opened more presents. A huge bar of his favourite Bourneville chocolate, some navy blue slippers, and a pack of Karate shower gel, soap and deodorant. "Do you *have* a shower?" asked Myra. There wasn't a shower at the bungalow. Her father didn't answer. She tried again. "Do you have a bath or a shower?"

He didn't answer. What he did say was, "You've done me really proud. I'm going to document all this and give it to people less fortunate than myself."

"Oh, God!" said Myra, not meaning to speak out loud.

The day before her father left his home for good, he sat with Myra on the sofa. He'd been a member of the Rossendale Male Voice Choir. They listened together to a tape of him singing.

'*There is nothing like a Dame, nothing in the world.*

There is nothing you can name . . .'

Myra sang along with Harry to the next song.

'*Mud, mud glorious mud. Nothing quite like it for cooling the blood. So follow me follow . . .*'

"How do you know this?" he asked. "From school?"

"No. From listening to the tape. You gave me a copy."

"Did I?" he looked into the middle distance, then back at her. "You know I'm losing my reason?"

"Yes. Do you mind?"

"Not really. As long as I can keep going."

"What keeps you going?"

"Things that need doing."

Every few minutes her father would go into the kitchen and ask her mother, "Anything outstanding?"

"He talks to himself now," her mother said to Myra in a conspiratorial tone.

He wandered from room to room, less and less able to focus on an activity or a thought; he watered the pan stand instead of the plant stand; he poured milk into the sugar bowl. When he got ready for bed he put his vest over his shirt and his pyjamas over his vest. There was talk of a night sitter. Myra began saying and doing things she didn't normally do or say. She would kiss his forehead and hold his hand. She would say 'Take care' and 'God bless' when she left him.

But the next day he fell and cracked a rib. After six weeks in hospital he deteriorated so much that returning home was out of the question. The staff at Gorsey Clough tried to reassure Myra that her father was reasonably happy. "He makes me laugh," said Peter. "He came up to me the other day and said, 'Where's the main switch?' When I said I didn't know he said, 'Well, you're no use to me', and walked off."

"Does he seem settled?" asked Myra.

"I think so. Mind, they're all on a mission. Every so often they decide to escape. They all get up and surge to the front door. Then they go and sit down again."

Peter popped his head round the door. "Would you like to eat in here. We could set up a table. It'd be no trouble."

"Yes, please," said her mother.

Myra was relieved. At least they would have some privacy. She hadn't relished the thought of eating in the second lounge with the other residents.

A procession of trolleys, tablecloths, crackers and cutlery arrived. Peter laid the table, rearranged the chairs and placed plastic glasses next to the red napkins. Then he closed the window. While they waited for the food, Myra pulled a cracker with her father.

"Pull. Pull hard," she reminded him. He put on his yellow crown and Myra read out the joke, "Why did the boy put his granddad in the fridge?" No one offered an answer. "Because he fancied an ice-cold pop."

Her father drained his wine as though it were lemonade. When the food arrived it did its best to avoid his knife and fork. Sprouts tumbled off his plate; an angel on horseback fell to the floor. He put down his knife and fork and lifted a thin slice of turkey to his mouth. "Not with your hands," said Myra sharply. She couldn't bear to see the last traces of civilized behaviour slip away from him.

"No, daughter," he said. She took a spoon and began to feed him.

"You shouted at me when I did this at home," she reminded him.

"Still friends, though," said her father.

By twelve forty-five they had finished their meal. Myra opened the window. The fields stretched away to the foothills of the Pennines. Holcombe Hill rose on the horizon with its sturdy stone tower. Myra and her father had walked up that hill, down it, along it and beside it. He could still see the tower. Myra didn't know if that was a comfort to him or a torment.

"I rather like my family," he said. "But I hated their guts when they started to move away. It's chaos in here. Routine, routine, routine. Get you up in the morning, put you to bed at night. Breakfast, dinner and tea. Breakfast, dinner and tea." He turned to her mother. "You don't come very often." Her mother bowed her head and looked down at her lap.

Myra felt for them both. Her father spent large tracts of time away from those he loved. Her mother had lived with her father for forty-eight years and now she saw him once a week, if she was well enough. Her father didn't understand how her mother struggled through each week, besieged by the home helps, the district nurse, the chiropodist, the physio; if it wasn't the hairdresser at the door, it was the cleaner, the gardener, the Teleshop food delivery or the travelling librarian.

He talked on, making less and less sense. "I think about getting a carrot off the floor. We could do with a bit of hardboard between here and knitwear." Finally, he got up and wandered into the lounge, first making sure that he had a pocketful of chocolate.

Myra and her mother followed and sat beside him on the quadrangle of chairs. A woman was having an argument with the Christmas tree. Another was shouting over and over, "Nancy! Nancy! Will you come down? Mr Carr is poorly!" Three ladies sat looking very serious in winged armchairs, each with a black eye. A young girl ate scraps off the tablecloth and the floor, then tried to eat a small glass tree in a pot. She was there by mistake. Peter told Myra that when she arrived she had a life expectancy of three months. That was ten years ago.

Her father said to Myra, "I must keep in touch with the outside world. What is your address? What is your phone number?"

By the time Myra and her mother left he had begun to nod off.

That evening, after a long dose of television and two glasses of Advocaat, her mother said to Myra, "Thank you for making Christmas vulnerable." She paused. "Bearable, I should say."

When she visited her father on her own on Boxing Day, Myra asked him what had happened the day before. "We didn't have turkey," he said.

"Did you get any presents?"

"Bits of things. From China. My family came."

Myra picked up a pack of six substantial tumblers and took them to the checkout. She wanted glasses which wouldn't break easily. The assistant packed them carefully in tissue and dropped them into a large carrier.

She found her car in the multi-storey and headed north, towards home. It was dusk. The light was slipping between gentian and prussian blue. Myra remembered a turning off the main drag which passed a piece of derelict land. One wall remained from a bulldozed row of houses. She parked the car so that it faced the wall and left her lights on.

Taking the carrier, she stood between her car and the wall, and one by one she hurled the glasses. Each time she threw harder and aimed higher so she could see the glass skitter down the wall. The crashes were loud and satisfying. She stood for a minute then drove home, with little respect for the speed limit.

The house was dark, but David was home—Myra had seen his car parked outside. She climbed the stairs and peeped into the bedroom. He was lying on top of the duvet; his eyes were closed, his breathing deep. She lay down next to him and unbuttoned his shirt. Her fingers threaded themselves through the thick hair on his chest. His skin warmed her hand.

SWAN

IN THE CLASSROOM MARY tended to look baffled. Teacher after teacher tried to bring her out, bring her on, interest her in this aspect of geography or that approach to maths. But classrooms didn't appeal to Mary. She liked the garage and the river.

The river was a bicycle ride away and the garage was at the bottom of their cluttered garden. In those places it did not matter that Mary had a statement of special needs, a classroom helper, and a file as thick as a doorway. She mended her own punctures, she packed her own picnics and she collected her own wood. The wood came from the beach. At low tide she could walk along the shale and the mud and pick up an old rudder or some deck planks. She liked to look across the river and draw an imaginary line along the top of the buildings—the warehouses, Canary Wharf, the spikes of the Millennium Dome. Then she would cycle back along the lower road to her terraced house.

She stacked the wood in piles, according to size. If it was sodden she would stand it on end along the long side of the garage.

"Mary!" shouted her dad. "Your dinner's ready." Mary locked up her bike and leaned it against the other long side of the garage.

Mary's mum had died when she was three. Mary had a sense of her—she was tall, she had hair which shimmered down her back, she laughed a lot. But most of her life she had lived with her father, Chas, and that was what she knew. She went inside and washed her hands.

"Ahh, dad. Not that soup again!

"One more helping, then it's finished." Chas was famous for his batches. Batches of bolognese, batches of chilli, batches of pea and ham soup. It was a practical solution to being a single parent and usually Mary didn't complain. But this soup had been going on for a week.

"Dad, can I go to Tricia's tonight?"

"Again? Have you been invited?"

"She won't mind."

Tricia was the daughter of a neighbour. Tricia's mum and Mary's mum had been good friends. They had looked after each other's children so that one could go shopping or swimming, or have an afternoon nap. But Chas was afraid that Tricia would get bored with Mary. Tricia had started to go out with boys; Mary didn't show the slightest interest.

"How's the herring gull coming along?" her dad asked.

"I've got the beak. Tail feathers are a bit tricky." Mary's voice was nearly always monotone except when she talked about birds.

"These evenings are so light. Why don't you make use of them?

"Oh please, dad. I can do that at the weekend."

"Just for an hour, then." Mary gave him a hug.

Tricia's mum opened the door. "Hello, Lovely. Tricia's getting ready to go out, but come in." She called up the stairs, "Trish, it's Mary!" There was no answer. "Why don't you go up."

Tricia was in the bathroom drawing round her eyes with a black pencil. "You look like an Egyptian," said Mary.

"I don't feel like one." Tricia didn't turn round, but talked to Mary's reflection in the mirror.

"What do Egyptians feel like?"

"Search me. But I bet they didn't have period pains and pimples."

Mary didn't know what to say. Her periods hadn't started and her skin was clear as an apricot. "Where are you going?"

"We're going up the park."

"Who with?"

"Paul Kennedy. 9C."

"I thought he was going out with Sandra Jameson."

"She dumped him last week."

"What will you do?"

"Sit on a bench and look at the view . . . I don't know!" Tricia was getting exasperated. "Look, I'm going to be late. I've still got to get changed. I'll knock for you in the week."

"What are you doing at the weekend?"

"I'm not making any plans. I want to see what Paul's up to."

"Oh, yeah."

Mary went downstairs and let herself out.

On Saturday Mary went down to the river. She needed to restock her woodpile. After locking her bike to the railings, she climbed down the cement steps to the beach. What she needed was chunky blocks about three feet long. She carried a saw in her rucksack for longer pieces. As she bent down to examine a promising plank, she could hear a beeping noise behind her. She turned round. A boy was standing beside her, swinging a metal detector.

"Didn't mean to scare you," he said.

"You didn't," said Mary.

"This is a Bounty Hunter Junior. Got it off eBay." There was a pause. "What are you looking for?" he asked. Mary still didn't respond.

"There's lots of wood on the other side of that pier," he said, pointing downriver. Mary nodded but didn't meet his eye.

"I come down here every Saturday. I've not seen you before."

"I've not been for a while," Mary mumbled.

"Oh," he said and wandered off down the beach, his detector hovering a few inches above the surface of the mud and shale.

Mary watched him from the corner of her eye. She thought she knew him from school—Year 10, usually on his own in the playground. Steve or something. When her rucksack was bulging with wood, she made her way to the steps. As she pulled the handlebars away from the railings, Steve caught up with her.

"Get what you came for?" he asked.

"Yeah."

"Maybe see you here again?" His voice was expectant. Mary looked down and nodded.

All day Sunday she shut herself in the garage. In the far corner was a stack of cardboard boxes and in each box was a bird. Mary didn't make exact carvings of starlings and swallows, she made an interpretation. She would sit and watch magpies for hours, studying their shape, their wing span, the length of their legs. Then she went back to the garage and began. She had an assortment of tools—knives, hammers, chisels and any implement from the kitchen or her dad's toolbox she could garner. When each bird was finished she wrapped it carefully in newspaper and placed it in a box. No one knew about her birds, except her dad.

What Mary didn't know was that several of the boxes were empty. Chas had seen an advert in the local paper—submissions for an art exhibition at the Woodlands Art Gallery. He'd taken up five of the birds to show the curator. At each annual show for local artists, one artist was always highlighted and had a room all to themselves.

A month later Mary received a letter. She read it out very slowly at the breakfast table, "*I am delighted to invite you to be our showcase artist for this year. Do please come and look at the space and let me know of any special requirements you might have.*"

"Dad?" She looked at Chas for an explanation. He simply smiled broadly.

It was three weeks before Tricia called round to see Mary. Tricia knew she'd cold-shouldered her and she wasn't quite sure how she would react. They sat stiffly in the front room.

"Paul dumped me last week."

"Oh." Mary didn't know what she was supposed to say. "He has cracked teeth."

"I liked his teeth."

"Oh." There was short silence. "I'm having an exhibition."
"What of?"

"Birds. I make them. Want to see?" Mary unlocked the creaky garage door and unpacked a swift.

"You made that?"

"Yeah. Do you want to see another?"

Tricia held them carefully in her hands like newborn babies, one at a time: a heron, a sparrow, a jay . . .

On the day of the opening Mary had her long hair cut into a crisp bob. She walked arm-in-arm with her dad up the driveway to the gallery. There were already groups of people standing on the lawn sipping glasses of wine. Through the window Mary could see her birds standing on plinths. The light was catching the wing of a swan in flight.

THE DEPUTY HEAD

THERE WAS HALF AN hour of the half term left to go. Ed walked down the corridor to his room. Windows ran floor to ceiling along one side and he could see rows of unremarkable houses ranked beyond the playground stopping sharp at the foot of Shooter's Hill.

A queue of boys waited outside his door. "Brendan, what are you doing here?" Ed liked to be on the attack from the very beginning.

"Mrs Siddons sent me, sir."

"For a very good reason, I've no doubt."

"Sir," Brendan answered, casting his eyes to the floor in mock humility.

"Kilroy, I despair of you."

"Yes, Mr Banks." The boys knew that submission at this stage was the quickest way to escape; phone calls and letters home could come later.

"Let's have you in then." Ed unlocked his door. His room was organized into piles. He knew exactly where everything was. SATS test results, attendance records, accident reports—he could lay his hands on anything, just like that. His home was much the same.

Just now his front room was layered with piles of ironed clothes waiting to be packed—short-sleeved shirts, long shorts, short shorts, T-shirts. He was only going for a week, but October was so humid in Bangkok that it was impossible to dry clothes out on the balcony.

"Sit down, Brendan McLeish. What were you doing this time?"

"Turning on the gas taps."

"Dangerous as well as stupid!"

"Yes, sir."

Ed took his report card and began to fill in the details. Brendan gazed at the photographs on the walls—enlargements of young, brown-skinned men with sleek black hair. They were riding elephants, sailing down rivers, posing against backdrops of rounded mountains and paddy fields. Each young man was carefully framed and placed on the peeling almond-painted walls.

"You'll be on report after half-term."

"Yes, sir."

"How many times is this?"

"Don't know, sir."

"And I don't expect this will be the last. If you make me miss my plane, it won't just be report cards I'll be signing."

"No, sir, it'll be our death warrants." Ed smiled dryly. There was comfort to be had in their familiarity with his routine.

Ed dashed home to pack his case as soon as the queue was done. The anticipation of his trip had woken him at three that morning. In the late afternoon he often lay on his bed in his Hilly Fields flat thinking of his room in Bangkok at the River View Guesthouse; the clothes rail with the occasional hanger, the heavy cream telephone on the length of cupboards, the floor-long, pale blue curtains missing a hook or two. He would wake there to the sound of woks being beaten into breakfast, and the engines of the longboats knifing through the water with their blue, red and orange flashes. If Dang was staying with him he would already be awake and washing the glasses in the communal bathroom. If it was Lex, he would sleep on late into the morning.

Ed woke from a doze. The lights inside the plane had already been dimmed. His headset had slipped off and he could hear one of Britten's *Sea Interludes* straining through the earphones. The stewardesses were answering individual requests for glasses of water and sandwiches. Ed started to read the in-flight information which was posted on the video screen in green and pink. *570 miles per hour, 34 miles per hour tail wind, 33,000 feet altitude, outside average temperature . . .* This was as much as he could read before the screen flicked to a promotion of the oncoming video.

Electric storms were staining the clouds on the horizon into brown mountains. An orange moon hung beneath the wing of the plane. The stars had spilled into the cities and were stitched along streets and highways.

Ed knew Bangkok well. He'd made the trip to Thailand every holiday for the past four years—Christmas, summer, Easter and all the half-terms in between. "Such a lovely place to be," he told his colleagues at school. "He's got relatives there," said Beryl, his ally in the maths department. A wall of humidity hit him as the automatic doors pulled apart and he walked out of the air-conditioned airport building. He ignored the taxi touts, the invitations to the Oriental, the Royal Orchid Sheraton, the Shangri-La, and went straight to the bus stop.

He had to stand for part of the way, but he could see the trucks carrying bananas and pineapples; the taxis with red, yellow and white garlands swinging from their rear view mirror—roses, marigolds and jasmine threaded for luck; the sun blazing on the frequent gold on the temples.

Instead of changing buses, Ed hailed a tuk-tuk. He only had a week after all and what was eighty bhat? A couple of quid? He clung to the metal rail beneath the roof as the driver swung round the corners and sped up to the traffic lights.

Determined to walk the last few minutes of the journey, he stopped the driver, dragged his two bags onto his shoulder and slid off the seat. His guesthouse was on the edge of China Town. He wanted to savour the approach along the soi which he had come to know so well—the shop-houses, the piles of second-hand axles and wheel rims which were beaten all day for re-sale, the spirit house where he'd once seen a rat feasting on the offerings of mooncakes and oranges.

He stood a moment watching the pillars of ice being fed into a crunching machine. Maybe he'd invest in a bucket and have his whisky chilled. There wasn't a fridge in his room at River

View, but he was prepared to forgo that luxury for its situation on a curve of the Chao Phraya River. The room he always booked —Room 41, fourth floor—had views to the north and to the south.

"Sawat dee kha. Nice to see you again, Mr Banks."

"Sawat dee khrup. It's great to be back."

The reception area was swamped with Scandinavians, so Ed took his key and summoned the lift. The hallway on the fourth floor was newly swept and the saucers underneath the four identical pot plants were swimming with water. He unlocked the door and went to sit on the warm sofa on the balcony. There was a small yellow tug pulling three huge hippopotami barges towards the temple of Wat Arun. The river taxi swept past, a line of saffron monks sitting in the first seven windows.

Ed decided to go to Patpong as soon as the sun went down. He rather hoped that Lex would be in his favourite bar. Dang was cheaper, but Lex was younger and his skin was as smooth as a papaya. He was also a good teacher. It was much more fun learning Thai with Lex than with his tapes and phrase books.

He began to unpack.

SAYING GOODBYE TO THE ENGLISHWOMAN

HELEN HADN'T EXPECTED TO fall so totally in love—with the mist which rose each morning to show the mountainsides dripping with vegetation, with the towels wrapped with casual style around the heads of the Karennis, with the meek and resolute spirit of a people driven from their country by tyrants. Helen had lived in Camp 5 for a year. She'd found the Karenni on the internet one Wednesday afternoon in November.

"I think I've got it," she told Richard when he got home from work.

"What's that, darling?" Richard put down his briefcase on the wicker basket chair.

"The subject for my research." Helen tried to sound neutral.

"Oh, good." There was a pause. "Are you going to tell me, or do I have to guess?"

"You won't be able to guess."

"So, come on!" Richard feigned impatience.

"The Karenni. Northern Thailand. An ethnic tribe from Burma. Karenni is the smallest ethnic state . . ."

"Thailand! That's bloody miles away. Hours and hours and days away."

"Well, *a* day." She looked pleadingly at her fiancé. "You knew it would be like this." She'd been dreading telling him. But what had come out in her voice was her excitement. "It'll be okay. We can write. I can phone sometimes. Just think—you can visit."

"I'm thinking," said Richard, hiding only a fraction of his dejection.

During her year in the camp, Helen decided to make the Karenni her life's work. She lived in their culture and absorbed their concerns. She wore a longyi and learned to speak both Karenni and Burmese. She even willed herself to get malaria—so strongly did she identify with their hardships. In exchange for being fed, housed and provided with a framework for her research, she taught English to Standard 9 and 10 students in the camp school. She would teach through the day and make notes during the night. She noticed on her first day in the camp that on the maps which hung in the biggest classroom, Karenni State was shown not as part of Burma, but as an independent state. This was the forty-ninth year of their struggle.

Helen's bamboo hut overlooked the Mae Surin River and the boarders' volleyball pitch. In quiet moments she watched the young men darting across the pitch, their caramel thighs gleaming in the sun. These men came from other camps which didn't have schools. They left their families behind to live and learn in Camp 5, returning home in the long holiday. Some came from so far away that they didn't risk going home in the holidays in case they couldn't get back.

Helen's final three weeks were caught before her like a fish, which, held too tight slips out of your hands and dives back into the river. She tried to savour certain moments. She watched the Karenni women washing their long black hair in the river; their hair becoming a treacle tail with the sun gleaming on its blackness. She listened to the sound of the cockerels which woke her each morning, the orchestra of tree frogs which guaranteed her sleep, and the chanting of lessons by the students at night when only candles lit the bamboo huts. In three weeks time she must go home, write up her Ph.D., live in her new home in Nottingham, and marry her fiancé who was waiting for her with a lawn mower and a kitten.

Her brother, Tom was on a trip from England to visit her. The Karenni boys in the camp marvelled at his height and the breadth of his shoulders. "How is he so big?" they asked when their volleyball game with him was over. "What can we do to make us big?"

Helen had travelled from the camp into the nearest town—
Mae Hong Son. She wanted to see her brother off on the first
part of his journey home. On day one of waiting for a truck to
return to the camp, Helen was sanguine. She made a call to
Richard. "Richard, it's me."

"Helen. How lovely to hear you. I've just got into work."

"How's things?"

"Well, fine. We completed yesterday and the removal company are on standby for Friday."

"I'm sorry you're having to do everything by yourself."

"Don't worry. Just come back in one piece. How's it going?"

"Not so good. There were seven villages burned over the border last week. Morale is pretty low."

"That's terrible. Where do they go—the villagers."

"Into the jungle. There are hundreds living there."

"Is Tom still with you?"

"Yes, but he'll be leaving very soon. My card's about to run
out. Sorry darling. Lots of love."

"And to . . ." The phone went dead. Helen sighed. She looked
across at the lake and at that moment the jet of the fountain
spurted forty feet into the air. The mountains made a soft collar
in the distance, darkening to slate blue as the light began to
fade.

"Well," she thought, "that's one appetite satisfied."

Helen ordered two ice creams at the lakeside restaurant and
wondered whether to buy one of the rather poor quality guitars
on sale in the high street for the students she was leaving
behind. Was it better to have a poor quality guitar than none at
all?

On day two of waiting for a truck she became fidgety. She
smoked a lot, chewed gum, and began to realize that she might
miss saying goodbye to Maesie. She knew he was planning
to leave the camp. Maesie was a student. Not one of Helen's—he
was too old for Standard 9 or 10; though some of her students
were older—the ones who had become soldiers before complet-
ing their schooling. Ordinarily, without the civil war, he would
have been at university in Burma. His English was conversation-
al, and over the months he had taken to visiting Helen more and
more frequently. She enjoyed his company. He had a gentle face

and brown eyes which she could never get to the bottom of. He was quite tall for a Karenni and didn't make her feel such a giant.

The week before they had stayed up practically all night talking. Helen sat on the verandah hugging her knees. Maesie lay propped up on his elbow with his feet tucked in the small of her back. "Should I move?" she thought. The Karennis often showed affection to their same sex friends, but man and wife kept their distance in public. Helen did not move.

Trucks to the camp were intermittent, to say the least. There weren't enough for each camp to have its own. One woman, who began haemorrhaging while giving birth in Camp 5, had to wait for a truck to return from the town. She died on the way to Mae Hong Son hospital. The baby survived.

On the third day of waiting Helen was beside herself. She wouldn't be able to prepare her students for their oral exams, she had doubtless missed Maesie, and the time left to her was running out fast, like sand through a spanned hand. She had worked so hard to have this time in the camp—planning, saving, and raising money for months; she wanted her leaving to be careful and considered.

Tom had given up waiting with her. There were only so many conversations they could have as they sat in the lakeside café. They had gone for their farewell meal at The Fern restaurant three nights ago. Tom took up tourist pursuits—riding an elephant, hiring a motorbike, visiting the Mae Pha Sua waterfall. Helen saw him as she was walking up the road by the lake. At the junction, where the garden centre's bougainvilleas line the pavement, he drove across the junction on his hired motorbike wearing a red helmet. He looked straight ahead, unaware of her. It was as though he had already left.

Helen sat on the wooden steps of the International Rescue Committee offices and lit her tenth cigarette. How many more days would she have to wait? She had walked the circuit from here to the market place via the Karenni Foreign Office and the Defence House continuously. Nowhere was there a truck, nor any news of one. At the Defence House sixteen Karennis were waiting. They cooked, they watched TV, they swept the floor, they slept on the floor.

Tears began to fall over Helen's cheeks. There wasn't any other part of her life which she couldn't plan, where she couldn't expect to keep to her intentions. She waited for a truck. The Karennis waited for a truck. The Karennis were used to waiting. They were waiting to return to their ancestral land.

The sound of an engine turned into the road. A white truck, bruised with mud from the three-hour journey from the camp, pulled up outside the office. Helen put her head on her knees in relief. When she lifted her head, Maesie was standing in front of her.

"We killed a duck for you," he said. "Two days ago. I waited for you to come back. Very late I waited." She offered him a cigarette and he sat down opposite her on the wooden deck.

"What are you doing here?" Helen inhaled deeply.

"I have to go to the student headquarters. About leaving the camp. They want to know if I'm going to Chiang Mai. They can give me contacts." Helen knew this would be the last time she would see him. After a few minutes he got up to leave, without any words of farewell. Helen's pleasure at seeing him was quickly displaced by a knot of misery. As he walked down the road he did not turn around. Was this the extent of his goodbye? After a year of friendship, was this the measure of how he felt about her leaving? Were the Karennis all so perfunctory with their goodbyes?

The truck was due to return to the camp at seven o'clock. There were only a few moments when she didn't think of Maesie. By the time she climbed in the back of the truck the light had gone completely. She sat on the sacks of rice and tucked her bag down the side of a drum of oil. Fourteen others joined her. They wedged next to each other so that they were buffered against the shocks of the track. The headlamps made a tunnel of light ahead, and before they reached the jungle Helen imagined she could see beyond to the curves of the mountains and the emerald paddy fields in the flatness of the valleys.

Augustino sat beside Helen. He had recently been appointed as the new camp school headmaster. There was a large metal hook where his left arm used to be. "You must be really pleased —about being headmaster," said Helen.

"Let's drink to it." Augustino pulled a half bottle of Mekon whisky out of his jacket pocket. "How are your students?" he asked.

"Fine. Except I've lost time for them. I'm supposed to be preparing them for their orals."

"Maesie has been talking with them."

"Has he?"

"Yes. I was in the truck with him this afternoon. He will be back in Camp 5 in a couple of days. He can help you again."

So their farewell was yet to come. Helen locked that thought away. She would allow herself to think about it again when she got back to the camp.

After crossing the Mae Surin River twenty times, the headlights shone into a bamboo village on stilts. Helen was the first one out at the border. She rescued her bag, waved as the truck drove off, and trod the sand of the volleyball pitch in her bare feet.

She stood in her bathroom hut, ladling cold water over her back. Through the gaps in the bamboo walls she could see her longyis, her T-shirts and underwear hanging the length of two washing lines. The two young Karenni women who lived with her had washed her clothes while she'd been away. They'd also hung the walls of her room with sheets of newspaper. As she lay down to sleep she could hear them breathing in unison in the room next door.

A REVOLUTIONARY WIFE

As usual, Rebecca expected too much. That Lian, a politician in exile from Burma, who had escaped with his life into the jungle, who knew when he was near the border because he heard dogs barking, who let his people eat before he ate, whose main concern was sovereignty for his tribe, would think to buy her a chocolate egg, as she had done for him, to give on Easter Day.

"Did you buy me anything?" she asked as they lay in bed.

"A small thing," he said in his soft voice. "I like being with you like this." His arm ran up and down her body, reminding them both of what was there.

"Let's have a bath together," suggested Lian. They were due at Rebecca's sister's for lunch—it was already ten thirty.

"We could do that tomorrow. It'll take them the best part of an hour to get to Wimbledon."

"I'm looking forward to seeing Sasha again."

"And her you."

Lian sat up in bed. "Do we have an obligation?" he asked.

"To do what?"

"Go to church."

"Depends how guilty you are feeling. My family don't go to church much."

"That helps me not to feel so guilty."

There was a fifteen-minute wait for a train at Honor Oak. It was one of those April days when the clouds bunch up and pour their rain at full pelt, then the skies clear and the blue and brightness are intense until the clouds mesh together again. They surfaced from the tube and picked their way along the identical terraced houses with their comforting front doors and phormium-planted gardens. When they arrived at Rebecca's sister's they were drenched. Sasha answered the front door. "Happy Easter!" she said, full with excitement. Sasha was six years old and tall for her age. Lian opened his arms and she ran to him.

"Hi!" his voice rang. Rebecca tried not to feel jealous, but she did. Lian never welcomed *her* like that. He was reserved, as were all his tribe. The Karenni women walked behind the Karenni men on their way to church. Men showed affection in public to men and women to women, but men and women together were demure and undemonstrative. Children were a different matter.

But Rebecca was glad that Lian could share her family, if only for a couple of days. His was hidden away back in Burma—a wife and three girls. Lian had waited till his youngest was eighteen before leaving. When *he* was eighteen his mother pleaded with him not to become a soldier. When he was twenty-six his girl-friend fell pregnant—it was the first time they had made love. He stuck with it, looked after his family, and became the fifth most important politician in his state. But now he was more use outside Burma than in, and less likely to be shot or imprisoned.

At first, when he escaped to a refugee camp on the Thai border, his wife was brought ceremoniously to him every few months. Lian told her he'd visited a prostitute in Mae Hong Son. He had to tell her because he needed to use a condom. He'd used two with the prostitute, but he knew that to be sure of his wife's health he must use one with her. She said if he ever went to a prostitute again she wouldn't come back to see him. She didn't come anyway—he hadn't seen her for seven years.

Rebecca and Lian hung up their coats in the congested hall cupboard and went through to the living room. Sasha sat at Lian's feet.

"Have you got any Easter eggs?" asked Rebecca.

"I've got one white one, one black. I mean dark. And one with Smarties in it," said Sasha.

"If you eat your lunch you might get another one," said Rebecca.

"And another one," said Lian, shyly.

"Do you want to come and see my room?" asked Sasha, looking up at Lian.

"Of course," said Lian, delighted to be asked.

"That didn't take long," said Lou, Rebecca's sister. Lian followed Sasha upstairs.

"How's it going?" asked Lou.

"Exhausted. Him more than me. We come back from meetings and he just sits in a chair with his eyes closed."

"Trying to block everything out?"

"Hoping I won't brief him about the next bit of his itinerary!"

"How are the meetings?"

"It's hard to tell. Everyone is very nice, and they listen, but I'm not sure how much good it will do. We sat in a room in the Houses of Parliament last week with the chair of the Human Rights Committee. She happened to say that she had to get back to her constituency that evening. Lian pointed out that he couldn't go back to his."

"Hmm. What can you say?"

"He says that the Burmese people think the military have made up Michael Aris's death."

"Aung San Suu Kyi's husband?"

"Yeah."

"Why would they think that?"

"They don't have any access to proper information."

"That's so weird . . . hard to imagine."

Rebecca walked over to the bookshelves and picked up a photograph of her and Lou sitting together under a towel on a busy beach. They were seven and nine years old. "Lian doesn't have any photographs of himself as a boy, *or* as a young man. The ones left in his house at Five Mile Village had to be destroyed."

"Security?"

Rebecca nodded.

Lunch was roast chicken with six vegetables. Lou sliced the meat from the chicken and handed it round. Rebecca served the vegetables and looked at the carcass sitting in the middle of the table. When she was in the refugee camp on the border she'd been invited to a Karenni teacher's hut to eat a duck. It was considered a great treat—there weren't many ducks in the camp and one was killed that evening and roasted over a fire. Six or seven men and women sat on mats on the floor and pulled the duck apart. The bones were put back on the plate. Once the duck was stripped, the Karennis picked up Rebecca's bones and chewed and sucked and licked them again until all the taste was gone. Rebecca felt she's been profligate with her portion.

After the chicken there was fruit salad for desert—Sasha's favourite. Lian's phone rang. "Hallo. Ahh!" Lian said with pleasure. He looked at me. "Friends from Australia." The conversation round the table stopped. Rebecca knew she should suggest to Lian he went out of the room to take his call, but she couldn't —she didn't want to embarrass him. They all listened to one side of a Karenni conversation. Rebecca had listened to many Karenni phone conversations. When Lian visited her at the River View Guesthouse in Bangkok, his phone was always busy. He would roll up his shirt over his tummy and back, flick off his shoes and stand on the balcony. Rebecca would look at him, silhouetted against the Chao Phraya River and its traffic. If it was around six, a huge orange sun would sink quickly behind the tower blocks. Always, before he came to bed, he folded his clothes over the chair and plugged in his phone to re-charge.

"Mum, shall I sing that song I learned at school?" asked Sasha.

"Go on."

Sasha stood up where she was and shimmied. "Head, shoulders, knees and toes, knees and toes, Head, shoulders, knees and toes, knees and toes." Everyone laughed and joined in for the repeat.

"Smart girl," said Lian.

The table was cleared of dishes. Rebecca produced a brown paper with a box shape inside. "This one's for you, Lou," said Rebecca.

"How thoughtful," said Lou.

"You mean you haven't got me one?" Rebecca said in mock indignation.

"Of course I have," said Lou, handing over a paper bag, also cornered from its contents.

"And this one's for you," said Lian, handing a small carrier to Sasha from under the table.

"Wow!" said Sasha with pleasure, peeping inside. "Chocolate buttons!"

Rebecca silently handed Lian her carefully-selected egg. It was a modest size, milk chocolate, which she knew he liked, and filled with praline. He made a little bow and nodded at the same time. "And these are for everyone," Lian said, placing a cellophane bag of small, foil-covered eggs in the middle of the table. Rebecca told herself not to be disappointed that Lian hadn't bought an egg specially for her.

At Christmas time, Rebecca had wanted to send Lian a bottle of Eau Sauvage aftershave. But when she imagined him opening the present in the camp she knew it was the wrong thing to do. None of the other two thousand refugees would receive presents. The day would be different only because of two attendances at church, and a slightly more elaborate meal than usual. Even when Lian had lived at home he and his family did not exchange presents; instead they sent a donation to the local orphanage. Rebecca wrapped up two small, glass candle holders in the shape of stars, a supply of small red candles, and a photograph of herself. She posted them off to the Mae Hong Son PO box number for the camp.

"Can we go to the park?" asked Sasha.

"We can take you," said Rebecca. "Give your mum some peace."

The path from the house was speckled with rain. Sasha ran ahead to show the way. Lian looked into every front garden. "No vegetables?" he said. "At home we have a kitchen garden." Rebecca remembered him telling her.

"Did you sell the produce?"

"Yes, people came to buy."

"And you have lemon groves."

"They smell so good."

The road rose up to the edge of the park, then a path led down to the playground. Pools of narcissus swayed on the banks, the blue of periwinkle glimmered from beneath the bushes. Sasha made for the sandpit. Rebecca sat on the little surrounding wall, but Lian went straight in with Sasha and helped fill buckets and make sand mountains. Sasha squealed as they bashed the mountains down and Lian laughed with her delight.

Rebecca knew that there was very little time in Lian's life for small pleasures. He was forever taking taxis, streaking up the Chao Phraya River or boarding planes to sympathetic countries. He spoke at meetings and conferences, lobbied politicians, and used every opportunity to make people aware of the plight of his people. If an important dignitary was visiting Bangkok he'd be at the airport at five o'clock in the morning to welcome them. He shared his home with five other revolutionaries. They slept on the floor—next to the fax machine and the computer, or out on the balcony when the air was weighted with humidity.

It was there that Rebecca had stayed for her last night in Bangkok. Lian gave up his room for her. For the sake of propriety he didn't want them to sleep together. "You are my revolutionary wife," he said, as he smoothed the mosquito net over his bed.

Rebecca had to tug Lian and Sasha away from the sand. "You can come back another day," said Rebecca.

"Ahh!" wailed Sasha. Lian ruffled her hair and pulled a forlorn face.

"We have to go?" he asked.

"It'll take a while to get back," said Rebecca.

"I just want to be naughty, and to play," Lian whispered in Rebecca's ear.

When they did leave Lou's house, the sky had lost its light. The streetlights glazed the puddles with orange and cast an arc of light over Lian as he walked down the middle of the road. "She could be a leader of my people," he said.

"Who?"

"Sasha."

"She's six years old! She doesn't know about your people."

"She will grow up to be a fine woman. She has passion and vitality. I would love her to live with my tribe."

Rebecca couldn't believe what she was hearing. "But she's my niece! I introduced you to her!" Rebecca didn't quite know why she had said that. Unless it was because she felt usurped by a six year old. "She's not going to travel thousands of miles to live with people she doesn't know. She has her family here, her school."

Lian sighed. "She's so direct. Straight away she invites me to her room."

'He's fallen for her,' thought Rebecca. 'He's fallen for a six year old girl who lives in Wimbledon.' Lian walked to the tube station with a lightness Rebecca had rarely seen. His face was ecstatic, he threaded his fingers across both hands. How could he think like this? Did his own daughters not show signs of leadership? Perhaps not. He'd talked about one who had made an unfortunate marriage, one who was pretty, one not so pretty. Maybe in his dislocated life it was natural to find a kindred spirit wherever he happened to be, and to imagine she could carry on his life's work.

As they travelled in the train Lian received another call. Rebecca looked out of the smeary window; they were high enough to look across at Southwark Cathedral before they entered London Bridge. The rain was still shining the platforms. Rebecca remembered that she needed to change the sheets. When his conversation ended, Lian translated. "A friend of mine was due to attend a meeting in Germany. I booked him a ticket via Poland. He's been arrested by the Polish police. I should have got him a direct flight to Germany." He stared at the seat opposite and Rebecca took his hand.

The rhythm of the train and the memory of the previous night sent shivers through Rebecca's body. In the face of injustice, her responses were relentless.

THE REAL ESTATE

MY FATHER SAT BOLT upright in his borrowed bed and opened his eyes wider than I'd ever seen them. Then he let out two yelps, like an animal wrenched from a trap. I replied with my own jagged cries, and with that anguished duet he was ripped away. His skin quickly lost its colour, but I carried on stroking his cold hand and kissing his waxy forehead.

I had visited my father in his nursing home for ten days. Each day when I left I knew I might receive a call to say he'd got worse, so I kept my mobile switched on day and night. When I arrived that morning and my battery was flat, the staff found me a charger. I picked up the phone from beneath the bed and called my brother. "They asked if you were coming up," I explained. "When I said 'no' they asked me to leave the room. They must have sat him up in bed. I came back in the room, and then he died. I think what they did made him die—not in a horrible way—it helped him. And me."

"I'll come up tomorrow," said George.

The staff came in to pay their respects. They were as tactile with him in death as they had been in life. I was grateful for their kind words. Here was the evidence that, despite his dementia, he had meant something to these people—they had loved him in their way, and he them. The housekeeper came up to me. "I want to give you a hug," she said.

I knew that I had now lost both my parents.

When the room emptied I looked round. There were

photographs of my mother in a wheelchair eating an ice cream in Wales; there was another of my parents' fiftieth wedding anniversary—their faces glowing from the candles on the cake. Presents of aftershave, pot pouri and face cloths were stacked on the shelves, and a large pack of Premier Elite Wipes lay on the windowsill. I sat a while, kissed my father one last time, and drove home to my parents' bungalow.

The only thing my father had ever mentioned about his funeral was that he wanted a Scottish piper playing *The Flowers of the Forest*. The funeral directors gave me four phone numbers of pipers. None of them were Scottish. I booked one from Eccles. The others were either out, or unsuitable. One went into minute-by-minute detail about where he would stand, what he would do and what he would play. The other offered a more expensive package which included playing a quieter set of pipes at the house afterwards. He said, "You don't want to be tripping over a piper while you're filling your plate with quiche and potato salad."

Two years previously my father had watched from the hearse as his wife was buried; it had rained incessantly and the ground was too muddy for him to walk to the grave. Now his coffin was being lowered on top of hers. The funeral director had refined the procedure since my mother's burial. Instead of just the vicar throwing soil, the funeral director now approached our family, one by one, with a shepherdess wicker basket. I reached for a handful from the black mound and noticed specks of dandruff on the shoulders of his coat.

After my mother died I photographed each room of the bungalow—the layers of cards and letters in the letter rack; the arrangement of brush, comb and hand mirror on the dressing table; the baskets of dried flowers and the flanks of unused electrical equipment in the kitchen. The bungalow had stood more or less empty for those two years, apart from visits to my father, Christmas and bank holiday breaks, and the managing of the renovation.

The woodchip paper had been shaved from the walls and replaced with flat planes of 'Lavender Haze', 'Tealight' cream and 'Tailwind' blue. The airing cupboard had been stripped from the bathroom and a pristine white suite installed with an easy-to-manage shower. The 'Naples' yellow kitchen I'd chosen changed over the day, from the morning sun streaming through the window, to the evening when the theatrical ceiling spots pooled light onto the surfaces.

My brother had overseen the rewiring, the rebuilding of the garage and the filling of holes in the roof; he'd bricked up a window in the kitchen to allow for more units, and he'd oiled the beech wood work surfaces three times so that splashes of water stood proud.

At the start of the renovation I arrived at the bungalow after a long drive from London. I opened the front door to a belt of acrid smoke. George was up a ladder in the kitchen. There was a small fire beneath him on the dining table. "What's happened?" I asked. He was holding a blowtorch.

"I'm trying to get this glue off." There were burnt patches across the ceiling where he'd removed the glue which had held the polystyrene tiles. A burning globule had fallen down onto a tea towel on the table.

Now, with only the carpets left to replace, I invited three estate agents round. Would this mean that I could buy a bigger place in London? Would it mean that my brother could build his extension? The first agent arrived in a curvy silver car wearing a shiny grey suit; his glasses had a thin black bar across the top of each lens. He showed himself round.

"We've done everything bar the carpets," was my opener.

"Nice colours and nice colour changes as you walk through. I would clear the house of furniture, so it's like a show home. People can imagine their own stuff—you know, my sofa could go here, my dining table there . . ." His tone was measured and upbeat. "And if I were you, I'd do the carpets. Everything else is fresh and new and then your eyes go down . . . You could get a contract carpet for a thousand pounds—it would add five thousand to the value." He paused. "Biscuit—keep it neutral." I nodded.

"What price are you looking for?" he said, meeting my gaze.

"What would you say?"

"Two hundred and fifty. You'll struggle to get any higher because of stamp duty. They'll want you to come down, or they'll ask *you* to pay the stamp duty."

"They do that?"

"Oh, yes. Or they'll ask you to go halves."

"Would you go any higher than two-fifty?"

"Two-sixty . . . two-seventy-five tops."

"Hmm. Any other advice?"

"Will I offend you if I'm honest?"

"No."

"It's your soft furnishings which let you down. Curtains," he said as he stood in the big bedroom. "Nets are old fashioned." I had washed them for the spring. We walked through into the lounge. "That blind is really a kitchen blind."

"It was my mum's pride and joy." I remembered her pleasure at picking out the repeating pear and plum fabric.

"Oh well, leave that." He paused. "I do two properties a year."

"Do?"

"Do up, renovate. I love kitchens—granite and stainless steel. We've just got a new one at home."

"Do you cook?" I asked.

"I made a fish dish last week. I like getting everything out and making a mess." He looked out of the front window. "It's nice to see established trees and shrubs. Is that an acer?"

"Yes," I said. It had been planted to commemorate my niece who died aged three of a congenital heart disease.

"Your generation, your parents' generation—they garden. I'm just getting into it." I had never been referred to before as belonging to a particular generation. When did one generation stop and another start? I didn't see myself as necessarily that much older that this man. Perhaps he'd made an assessment of the generations from the line of family photographs on the mantelpiece.

On the doorstep he turned to me. "I hope this doesn't sound patronising, but you've done sterling work with this renovation. Phone me if you've got any other questions."

An hour later the second agent arrived. His vehicle was a 4 × 4 and his suit dark blue.

"I wouldn't bother to change the carpets," he said. "Let them choose their own. Leave some furniture and then organize a van to clear it when it's sold. We've got some phone numbers."

He was altogether more formal than the previous man—

older, with rimless spectacles. He stood in the hall and started to point his electronic measurer. I stepped into the bathroom to get out of the way. Behind him on the wall was a black and white photograph of my father, looking particularly handsome with his hair brylcreamed into a wave. The agent didn't measure any other rooms but made his way into the kitchen. I offered him a straight-backed chair.

"Is this your chair?" he asked, "I don't need a cushion." I wasn't sure if he was being polite or fussy.

"I'm tall as well," was all I could think to say.

"We can arrange block viewings. We could get fifteen people at a time!" I imagined fifteen prospective buyers milling around the bungalow; fifteen people imagining themselves relocated to this home I'd been visiting for twenty-five years.

"What price are you after?"

"What would you say?"

"Two hundred and fifty."

"Would you go any higher?"

"No," he said abruptly. It was obvious there wasn't going to be any explanation to follow.

"What do you want the money for?"

"We're not sure, really," I said, and smiled.

"Is that everything you want?" he asked.

When he got to the doorstep he turned to me. "Do you have gas central heating?"

"Oil," I said.

"Is there gas up here?" I reassured him there was.

As he accelerated out of the drive the phone rang. It was George. "How did it go?"

"We're not having him," I blurted out. "He can sod off! He wanted to know what we want the money for!"

"Why!" said George. I updated him with the conversations so far.

The third agent came the following afternoon. I had already received a letter to say that Marsha Wilcox would be arriving at 2:30 p.m. and she would be very happy to talk to me about marketing opportunities. Marsha wore brown flowing trousers and a cropped jacket. She drove a contemporary jeep. "Preston and Wilcox," she announced when I opened the door. She wanted to see the full extent of the property inside and out, including the garage. "Lovely plot," she said, "nice and private."

"You smell nice—what is it?" I asked as I lifted the garage door.

"Everyone says that. Calvin Klein Euphoria."

It wasn't until she was sitting on the sofa that Marsha really got started. She opened a company folder. "Your information would go into all our four offices." She pointed at the photographs of their window displays on the back of the folder. "Our marketing is second to none. We're on all the national websites —which is where we get most of our interest. Keep some furniture and leave the carpets as they are—you won't gain anything by replacing them. I'd say two-fifty."

"You wouldn't go any higher?"

"You could do 'offers over'. That way buyers would know you're serious about the two-fifty. But any higher and people want a better kitchen and bathroom. When were you thinking of selling?"

"Well, it's my parents' home. They don't live here any more. My father died in January."

"I know what you're going through. My mum died when I was twenty-two. I cried for three years. I still can't have a photograph of her anywhere near me."

"I'm sorry," I said.

"She was forty-six. Heart attack. I used to get out of bed and go down to the kitchen and cry into a tea towel—I didn't want my partner to see me. After three years I realized I was crying for myself, not for my mum. You know—if I'd had a bad day."

"But you have to grieve," I said.

"If I had a good day I didn't cry for her. So I stopped. So I know how hard it is."

"Would you put it on at two-sixty?"

"If that's what you want. But really, people are going to come in here and say, out with the fireplace and out with the conservatory."

"I've never really liked that conservatory. But my parents did." They would entertain in there with the Royal Albert tea service and a plate of egg custard tarts. Even when dad was quite ill, he laid new tiles on the floor.

"It really wants pulling down and building again. Even if you tidied up the garden—really cut it back . . ."

"Believe it or not, we've spent quite a lot on the garden." Mum wasn't a tidy gardener. She preferred the privacy of tall trees. She hung baubles on an evergreen shrub at Christmas, and each night she brought in her two plaster doves to shelter in the porch.

"We don't do block viewings." Marsha looked disgusted at the thought. "We attend every viewing personally. When you're ready, get in touch."

We shook hands on the doorstep.

Later that afternoon I phoned my brother. "We have to be sure this is what we want to do," I said. "Once it's sold we can't buy it back."

"I thought you needed the money."

"I thought *you* needed the money."

"Not really. I'm happy enough where I am."

"Well, we can do without an extension."

"I just like being here," I said, knowing now that this was what I wanted. "I brought in the washing this morning and I remembered how mum would be sitting in the kitchen, wanting everything in its place—every knob on the cooker pushed in."

"I know."

"Shall we keep it then? See how we feel in next spring?"

"Yes, let's do that."

I phoned the flooring men who had fitted the bathroom and kitchen vinyl the morning my father had died. We had talked about the possibility of carpets. I would get them done. We could enjoy the feel of them beneath our feet for a whole year.

ACKNOWLEDGEMENTS

Sandshift won second prize in the Southampton Writer's Conference short story competition, 1990; *A Small Smudge of Blood* was one of the six equal winners in the ICA *New Blood* short story competition, 1996; *Treatment Room* was a prizewinner in the *Biscuit Fiction* 2002 competition; *A Small Smudge of Blood* and *Lady Macbeth* were highly commended in the creative non-fiction category in the 2006 New Writing Ventures Awards.

Between Here and Knitwear, Family Connections, Matilda and One of the Twelve Dancing Princes, and *Treatment Room* were broadcast on BBC Radio 4. These stories and others were first published in *Adrift from Belize to Havana* (Biscuit), *Breakfast All Day, Cadenza, How Maxine Learned to Love Her Legs* (Aurora Metro), *Northwords Now, The Interpreter's House, The Printer's Devil, The Reater, Orbis, QWF, Signals 3* (London Magazine Editions), and on Laura Hird's *Showcase* website.

With thanks to Spread the Word for funding a critique with the Literary Consultancy in 2001, to Hawthornden Castle for a fellowship in 2001, to the Royal Literary Fund for financial support in 2002, and to the Arts Council for a Grant for the Arts in 2005 to complete this collection. The extract from the poem *My Lover* is reproduced by kind permission of Wendy Cope. My special thanks to Alison Fell for her creative writing classes at City Lit.

Printed in the United Kingdom
by Lightning Source UK Ltd.
123494UK00001B/114/A

9 781844 712984

Index